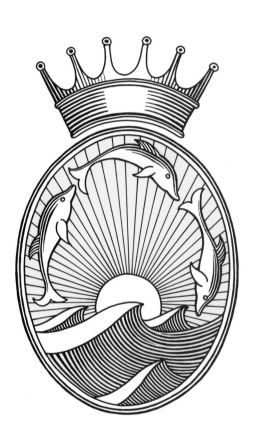

A CITY IN WINTER

A CITY
IN WINTER

MARK HELPRIN

ILLUSTRATED BY

CHRIS VAN ALLSBURG

VIKING • ARIEL

On page 47 note that the description in the third paragraph is a direct quote from *Webster's New International Dictionary*, 8th ed., Springfield, under "yam."

VIKING
Published by the Penguin Group
Penguin Books USA Inc., 375 Hudson Street, New York, New York 10014, U.S.A.
Penguin Books Ltd, 27 Wrights Lane, London W8 5TZ, England
Penguin Books Australia Ltd, Ringwood, Victoria, Australia
Penguin Books Canada Ltd, 10 Alcorn Avenue, Toronto, Ontario, Canada M4V 3B2
Penguin Books (N.Z.) Ltd, 182–190 Wairau Road, Auckland 10, New Zealand

Penguin Books Ltd, Registered Offices: Harmondsworth, Middlesex, England

First published in 1996 by Viking, a division of Penguin Books USA Inc.

1 3 5 7 9 10 8 6 4 2

LIBRARY OF CONGRESS CATALOGING-IN-PUBLICATION DATA
Helprin, Mark.   A city in winter / by Mark Helprin ;
illustrated by Chris Van Allsburg.   p.   cm.
ISBN 0-670-86843-4 (hardcover)
I. Van Allsburg, Chris.   II. Title.
PS3558.E4775C58   1996   813'.54—dc20   95-49579   CIP

Printed in Italy
Set in Caslon 540

LIST OF ILLUSTRATIONS

For Alexandra & Olivia
M.H.

I went down to the city on the plain when I was not yet ten years old, only a short time after I had discovered who I was and whence I had come. My story is simple, the story of struggle, so well known to all who come into this world, and I am writing for you, my son or daughter not yet born, so that you too may know who you are and whence you have come. Listen to the tale, which is also yours, and is told for love. Come back to me, come back to this time before you were born, to a golden morning in December as the sunlight frosts the city roofs, and a thousand singlets of smoke rise to the pure blue heavens in which I place my trust.

I rightfully inherited the throne of this kingdom and empire from my parents, who had been dispossessed, but I had to take it as well, and in the taking and in the years before, I was a child of the poor, I lived in the mountains, I knew war. These are the things that have made me, and I cannot ever leave them behind.

We fought in the highlands, the forests, and on the plain. The city itself was a battleground (first when we besieged it, and then when we defended it), and during the initial years of the revolt the wind often brought the smell of smoke from burning houses, streets, or whole districts. Archers would strike at their pleasure, extinguishing lives as if they were at target practice. And for years the wooded areas within the city walls were crowded with refugees in shantytowns where fires burned all night but were never quite strong enough in winter to keep the children warm. From the palace, their deficiencies unknown, the fires looked merely beautiful.

Though I myself have seen so many battles I can hardly tell one from another, far worse than any battle was to take leave of your father when he left to fight. All the suffering of these years seemed to lie in the moment when our outstretched hands would part and either he or I would turn to ride away. Even now he is riding with the Damavand, the horsemen from whom I am descended, whose land is on the outer reach of the kingdom as it vanishes into the Veil of Snows. Detachments of soldiers and caravans of merchants who fall into the Veil of Snows may be lost forever, or may return in confusion years later, knowing neither where they have been nor for how long. Those who come back seldom are remembered, for by the time they return, no one of their generation remains.

Though Damavand generals sometimes drive their enemy deep into the turbulence of the snows, they cannot pursue. Should they spur their horses into the looming gorges or out onto the infinite snowfields, they simply disappear.

Your father is now with the armies in the high peaks of the Damavand. I learned from having fought in the last great battle, at the edge of all we know, that when you ride in the shadows of those mountains something in your heart draws you to them as if they were black water flowing hypnotically beneath a bridge. Once you have ventured into that country, only if you have a great deal of life in you can you resist going too close, for as you lift your head to stare at clouds of ice swirling above blinding snowfields, you feel as pleasurable a tide as if you were standing in the surf in June.

When you ride with Damavand cavalry, time has no meaning, life flows with the speed and power of a mountain torrent, necessity dictates all, and the heart is keyed to the blood of horses that canter for days in wind and snow. In the last battle, your father and I commanded the two armies that harried the battalions of the usurper, a man, my ancient enemy, whose name I will neither utter nor write. That I will never say his name I promised to the tutor, who taught me not to dwell on evil. Who is the tutor? You owe your life to him, as I owe mine.

In the last battle we pushed the usurper's soldiers so hard against the Veil of Snows that their formations melted into the ice, their ranks were eaten by mist, their cries swallowed by silence. We fought so close and so fiercely that we lost track of time, and we watched as half our soldiers passed from this world into the world of the wind.

And at the very end my heart grew still as I stood on a distant crest while your father and the usurper fought upon a high cornice half hidden by curtains of glassy snow. Blinded by sun flashing against snow and ice, I thought your father would be taken to the other side, but as he fell and the usurper was about to strike, a tongue of ragged cloud swept across them, luffing the usurper's black robes, and when the field was white again and shone with sun, only your father remained.

This was our blessing, but it was just the last of many gifts of providence, and, like all good things, impermanent. As stars rise, they fall, and as they fall, they rise, which is why your father has encamped with thousands of horsemen in the valleys near the tree line and the high lakes. He watches even when it seems that nothing will come, for we ourselves have seen that fortune does not stick in place, and the prospect of your birth has driven him to great care.

Now the snow that when I was young rushed past my face like maddened swarms of insects lies quietly upon my palace roofs, dampening footfalls below in halls of marble and softening the noise from courtyards as large as city squares. Streams of smoke from my chimneys rise peacefully and straight.

It was not always as it is. Not long ago this dream of peace moved me so as the object of my prayers that I grieved for it as if for a lost love, but now that I have it in hand the days of war flood upon my memory in honor and grace.

Why have I spent my life at war? Why does this time of peace seem unnatural? And how did all this come to pass? Through love, and loyalty, and memory that reaches into places I have never been.

Until my ninth year I lived in perfect innocence in a perfect place. The air was clear, the sun shone bright, and the hay was dry and blond. It all might have remained that way, but as soon as my heart began to stir and I began to wonder about the city on the plain, the tutor broke the undisturbed perfection and told me my history, as if to see me born before his eyes.

My father, he said, was the heir to the throne, and my mother a princess of the Damavand whose parents had been murdered by the usurper when she was an infant. Slain by archers in the courtyard of an inn, my grandparents had covered my mother with their bodies as they died, and because she was inexplicably silent, the assassins thought they had killed her.

But she was unhurt, and a maid at the inn retrieved the baby and carried her deep into the forest. She was never to return to the country of the Damavand. Nor was she ever to set foot in the city from which she had been spirited. Instead, accident and fate brought my father to her in the forest—my father, who was a prince, and she, who was a princess. But their time together would be short, for soon after I was born they, too, were murdered: the cause of the first war that split the kingdom. Pushed by a detachment of archers to the edge of a precipice above a lake, they chose to die in a fall rather than be pierced by half a hundred crossbow bolts.

I am, then, the second child who has not known her parents, the second child whose mother and father were taken from her by this same man whom we have now conquered but not killed, whom we have driven into the Veil of Snows, and for whom we watch day by day.

The maid who had saved my mother had to flee yet again. Knowing that I was her queen, she carried me into the South Mountains, where the Veil of Snows does not touch, where it is more beautiful and tranquil than language can describe, and where I spent my childhood with no hint of who I was or how I had come into the world. I was loved and I was happy, but though I was not yet ten years of age I knew that the heart needs a trigger of imperfection to be made whole. I hungered for the sight of a great thing, or the taking of a great chance, or the making of a great sacrifice.

The tutor, whom I called grandfather until the day I discovered that he was not of my own blood, knew that I would go. He knew that, once I had found out my past, love and loyalty would rise as if from nothing, and that I would enter a great city (I had never seen even a town) where as a ten-year-old child I would set about overthrowing a regime that enjoyed perfect and detailed control of absolutely everything.

When the tutor told the tale, I did not understand my part in it until the very end, but then all came clear. I could not have loved my mother and father more in the flesh than as they were presented in his story. Perhaps I loved them more because they were lost. As you will discover, the greatest love is for those who are lost.

How could I have left him, this man who raised me? How could I have gone to overthrow a king? How could I, so young? I don't know, but I began my journey to the city in blindness and confidence, which, if you think of it, is how we must all live, given the nature of our origin and the certainty of our destination.

I left in the fall, after harvest. I cried to leave the tutor, for, as he had vowed never to return to the city on the plain, I thought I might never see him again. I was afraid of the darkness and the road. I dreaded the wild boar, the wolf, and bear. And I had no idea what I would find in the city or what to do when I found it. But I left just the same. I had no choice. That I was so young did not matter. The usurper had forced the spirit of my family behind a high and heavenly dam, and when the dam broke, the spirit of my family came flooding down.

We were three days' walk from the nearest track. Guided by the North Star, I crossed the flanks of the mountains through tall forests dimly lit and over meadows above the timberline, where the snow can be a foot deep while on the plain the lakes are as warm as a bath.

In seemingly never-ending glades of birch and laurel I twice stumbled onto wild boar so much larger than I that I felt as if I were in the presence of a kind of whale. I had no strategy, no power, no recourse, and no retreat, so I did what I could. I scolded them for startling me, shaking a finger at them and slightly tilting my head as I spoke. And these creatures, who singly have destroyed squadrons of mounted hunters, bowed their heads and crouched as if they were shamed by my reprimand. Perhaps it was because, being less than an arm's length from the grotesque mouths out of which bristled their curling tusks, I was the first being other than those of their own kind who had actually looked deep into their eyes. Though it was many years ago, I remember that the eyes are as weak and watery as the body of the boar is strong and hard.

On my second day on the road I met a caravan of merchants

heading for the South Mountains, where they had never been. A dozen of them were traveling with a hundred snow-white mules—I had never seen a horse or a mule. They were so terrified of the great forests and high passes that had been my refuge, and so shamed by my cheerful assurances, that they offered me a mule on which to finish my journey.

"It will take ten days," they said, "to reach the city's south gates. The mule is slow and deliberate, but still faster than you."

So it was that I pacified wild boar, first saw a road, and entered the city. In my ten days' ride I had feared that the things that were happening to me had robbed me of my will and my power, for the road led, the mule carried, in the forest the weather had been compassionate, and the boar had slunk back as if behind me were an angel with a sword.

Never before had I been in a city. I was surprised to find that the walls and towers I had seen as I approached were not the only row of buildings, and that the city was deeper than it was wide. At first, things were not easy. For example, I had always greeted everyone I met. The tutor and Anna the maid were the only people I had ever known. In fact, except for a hunter who once stumbled onto our cabin when I was small, and the merchants I had just met on the road, they were the only people I had ever *seen*. So I politely greeted every person that I passed. As I encountered thousands upon thousands of people going about their business in the streets, I said, "Hello. How are you?" to each of them. It was exhausting, and because I was too young to have been a politician, they assumed that I was insane.

I said hello to everyone until I was too worn to speak, and no one, not one person, responded. Were it not for ruffians who pushed me and snatched at my dress, I would have begun to suspect that I did not exist.

So rapidly and completely assaulted were each of my senses that I hadn't the time to miss home. To right and to left, up and down, above and below, things were continually happening. I found this overwhelming, because in the forest things happened only every two weeks or so. Not here. Here, men swallowed fire and swords. I had never seen anyone swallow a sword: I had never seen a sword. Recreant women were placed in stocks and dipped in pools of icy water, their husbands tied to stakes while for a tenth of a gold Rothbart anyone who pleased could throw pies or fruit cocktails at them.

A thousand vendors lined each broad boulevard, and the whole city was a vast kitchen in which donkey meat, and wurst, and worse, were turned on rotisseries powered by sullen rats running on treadmills in pursuit of ever elusive chunks of Turkish taffy. The muskrat kebobs and crow nuggets were only part of it. On every corner, cauldrons competed to offer soups as fetid as infantrymen's socks, and treacherous pet handlers offered their birds or gerbils for frying, baking, or whatever you please. The selection was limitless. Eventually, I would hardly even take notice when at one stand or another whole woodchucks were consumed on the half-shell, as the vendor screamed, "The trick is in the sauce! The trick is in the sauce!"

Mad souls sold everything. They sold small ugly trinkets that did nothing, cloaks of painstakingly stretched bee hides, land in countries that did not exist, combination megaphones and dental picks, small creatures trapped in bottles, oics (whatever they were), pictures, elixirs, snapdragons, flagons, sponges, chariots, bells, mattresses, plungers, and lariats, folding furniture, singing lessons, chalk, rope, pigs, wigs, and weapons of war. The Tookistrasse was devoted exclusively to stores that specialized in only four items each. One, for example, sold Swedish medical books, lemons, arrowheads, and bassoons. Another sold balls of ambergris, pictures of ancient philosophers, chocolate pretzels, and wire mesh.

To scare up business, each storekeeper stood in front of his establishment and screamed about his wares until his eyes popped and his face was the color of a cherry. You knew that they had become so accustomed to this that they did it not because they wanted to sell their ambergris or gray flannel exercise pants but because they could do nothing else. In fact, on one of the streets that together led like a hundred thousand rivers into the palace square, I passed a great building that in other countries might have been a central post office or the ministry of the interior. Here, it was an old-age home for the merchants of the Tookistrasse and some of the other great commercial avenues, and its countless windows, rising hundreds of feet and extending along the length of a building that took five minutes to traverse at the pace of a mule trotting like a bug to its stable, were filled with ancient merchants still as red as cherries, eyes popped almost all the way to Bolivia, screaming automatically of latex carriage mats, nut bars, mechanical pillows, and nose-correction clamps.

And all this was but the prelude to the chaos, the color, and the music of the palace square at dusk. I didn't then know the meaning of hopelessness, or of desire, elation, or defeat. But when I felt them swirling together entwined in the open space above the square I understood immediately what they meant, as they fused into one strong cry of the heart. In the palace square the open space was like an ocean of freedom for a people otherwise oppressed, and the airy sea to which they came each evening to await events lapped against seemingly infinite walls of stone.

Here were defiance and freedom, but all in chains. And the two mixed like the warm currents of wind that spiraled up from the great bonfires and tumbled through the winter air.

Roman candles were launched from a hundred different points, exploding like the destruction of heaven, and drops of fire poured down from walls, towers, and the tops of trees. Who poured the flaming oils that hissed threats and dissatisfaction before they disappeared, and why? I never found out, and it has not happened since the rebellion.

Full orchestras played the remembered music of empire, music that was written no longer, and in one corner of the square a plain of ice that from high in the palace must have seemed no bigger than a speck held ten thousand delirious skaters gliding in unison to the music of an orchestra of at least half their number. Flames glowed from tripods set upon the ice in long lines that, like railway rails, came together only in

illusion. And here and there, in pockets of silence, a single couple might be seen, skating together through the shadows.

A million people were in the palace square, their upturned faces lost in a fume of luminous white that churned against the gray smoke of dusk. And here I left the snow-white mule, dismounting as he continued on, for I thought that I had found the center of the world.

As soon as I alighted I realized that music and the wind were not the only sounds I had been hearing. The streets were awash in whispering that sounded like the flow of water in small streams, or wind that lashes the pines and courses through their needles like sea foam. The whole nation had been put in exile by one man, and yet no one had gone anywhere. People spoke in short, clipped, guarded exchanges, or they whispered.

Given the nature of that which was cooked, it was hard to be hungry, but after a few hours wandering in the knee-high surf of whispering, and after following the motion of the skaters as they sailed in and out of flames and shadows with the damaged grace and dark electricity of the aurora, I was chilled and feverish and I desperately wanted something to eat. I had been in the freezing air for many days, and though the wind had made me strong and my eyes burned with the new, I wanted to come in from the cold.

Not only did I have no money, I had never seen money. Though the tutor had hurriedly explained it as I left, his thoughts were sometimes unduly compressed. Even if they were not like the mad whispering beneath the walls, they often eluded me. Money, as I understood it from his breathless dissertation, was defined primarily by its velocity. It was, like anything else, a commodity that rose or fell in value even if it were in itself a measure of value. The essence, he had said, was convertibility. This led him into a complicated essay on price theory. All very well and good, but I hadn't the slightest idea of what he was talking about.

When I came to a vast bakery in the open square I simply asked if I could have some bread. "As much as you'd like," said a man so strange that I couldn't take my eyes from him. He was tall and thin, with a bulbous, hooked nose, and shaggy camel-colored hair. His huge eyes were composed of concentric circles the color of tiger stripes, and every time he spoke he smiled. Though in the future he would protect me, I felt upon looking at his sloping shoulders and his gangly neck that, somehow, I had to protect him.

"I'll take ten, please."

"A quarter Rothbart and a tenth weasel gold ducat."

"What?" I asked.

He repeated the price as I stood in place, uncomprehending.

"Are you from elsewhere?"

I nodded.

"From the West Plain?"

"No."

"From the Prairie of Salt?"

"No."

"Uh, from the Gulf of Tizla?"

"No."

"From the forests?"

"Yes."

"A forest girl!" He was stunned. Virtually no one lived in the forests anymore, and those who did were valued as islands of tranquility, touchstones of the past, being completely ignorant of the troubles that had made life in the kingdom so ugly and bleak. Of course, I was not at all ignorant of these, but he could not have known that. "Wait," he said. "I'll get Notorincus. Meanwhile, eat." He pushed a tray of hot bread in my direction, and it held me in front of his stand like a magnet.

A loaf and a half later, he returned with Notorincus. I wasn't sure that, like the tall one, Astrahn, Notorincus was human. Whereas Astrahn was slim and buff colored, Notorincus was a squat, stocky ball, with rich black hair cut like fur. It did not lie or fall like human hair, but stood in palisades, as in a pelt or a cut rug. His eyes were slightly crossed, his face round. Most remarkable was his mouth, for this man who at first was too abashed to look anyone in the eyes had two glacially white beaver teeth in the center of his shy smile.

He was Notorincus, a bakery slave, and Astrahn was a slave's slave, which was rather low on the social scale but much in demand, as every slave wanted above all a slave of his own, and the masters, who were themselves slaves of the nobility, who were themselves slaves of the usurper, were happy to double their work force. Astrahn and Notorincus were two of a vast number of bakery slaves, of which at least a third were slave's slaves. The slave's slaves had been told that the usurper would soon establish a new position—the slave of the slave of a slave—and this kept them happy in their days as slaves of slaves.

But Astrahn and Notorincus were slaves only in name, for they had taken the oath of rebellion, something of which I had not even heard, something of which even the tutor had not heard, as it had been established long after his exile. Like the mad whispering, the oath moved no stones, burned no treasuries, and loosed no arrows, but it put the oath takers in a state of expectation and it freed their souls.

"Duck under the counter," Notorincus said. Never having heard this expression, I looked under the counter, expecting to see a duck. Then he said, "Come quickly." Though I wasn't sure that I should, I did. They took me closer to the ovens, and by the light of a myrrh fire they gave me soup and bread. They wanted news of the outside, beyond the struggle, news that I could not provide, because, as far as I knew, nothing had ever happened to me.

Had they asked me about myself, and had I been willing to answer, the rebellion might have started that day, and far too early. But they were caught in the wave of things, and they asked questions that did not lead home. Quite apart from that, the tutor had forbidden me to reveal who I was before the time was right.

"And when will the time be right?" I had asked.

His reply was, "When the whole people is like a great stone at the top of a hill, and it seems as if even the wind might rock the stone over the edge to begin its force-filled descent."

With no idea that Astrahn and Notorincus had taken the oath of rebellion, or even of the oath itself, I ate my soup and answered their questions not as if I were an owl but as if I were an otter.

"What forest did you come from?" asked Astrahn.

"The only forest I know, and I know only the forest."

"The forest of the South Mountains?"

"Where I started was for me the center. I have advanced from the center, but in which direction I do not know."

"Where did the sun come up as you made your way, on the right or on the left?" Notorincus asked, helpfully, and, of course, slyly. He turned deep red.

"It was cloudy."

"In what direction, then," Astrahn prodded, "was the North Star?"

"North," I said.

"Was it behind you? To your left? Your right? Ahead?"

This inquisition was child's play compared to the tutor's Pythagorean examinations. The tutor had been the chief of the

royal academies and libraries, and in my first nine years I had been his only student, the sole recipient of his discourses, and the lone disciple of his drills. Though I didn't know how lucky I was to be the single interlocutor of such a brilliant man, I did know a great deal else, from physics and mathematics to the history of art and the theory of music. Only in certain practical matters and in social discourse, for which we had no need in our splendid isolation, was I deficient. In answer to Astrahn's question I stated that "On some days, the North Star was on my right."

"Aha!" he said.

"And on some days, it was to my left."

"Oh."

"And sometimes it was behind me, though at other times it was in front."

"Oh, oh, oh," said Notorincus, his eyes more crossed than usual.

"Most of the time, though," I offered naively, as if to clinch the matter, "it was directly overhead."

"Well," Notorincus said, spreading his arms and turning up his hands, "tell us about the forests."

"Ah," I said, "they were beautiful."

"Is that all?"

"And they were green."

"Ask her about animals, Notorincus. You know about animals. You'll be able to tell that way."

"Good idea," said Notorincus, and then he cleared his throat. "Ahagghham! What animals lived in this green forest?"

"My!" I said. "So many animals."

"Tell us about them."

"My favorite," I declared, "was the spoffet-toed chowgis."

"I don't know that one," Notorincus said.

"We fished for mavrodaphnic seacats."

"In sweet water?"

"In brine wundels and sodium freshets."

"What about birds?"

"What about them?"

"Eagles, crows, owls, pigeons?"

"Let's see. Uh, no. Whistlenots, windowbangers, and monument foulers."

"Put it this way," Notorincus said to Astrahn. "If she's an agent of the usurper, his tactics have changed."

"All right," said Astrahn, "I agree. We'll get right to the point."

I sat coyly, saying nothing.

Astrahn turned to me. "Ahem!"

"Yes?"

"Were there armies of rebels in your neighborhood?"

"In the forest?"

"Yes."

"No."

"Were there . . . small bands?"

"No."

"Individuals?"

"No."

"Not a single rebel?"

"What are rebels?"

"Men that soldiers chase. Men who are hungry and tired and wounded. Men with scars and broken hearts and families destroyed or left behind."

"Once," I said, "a hunter came. He asked directions, and I gave him a bag of mushrooms."

"He asked *you* directions?"

"Yes."

"Good luck to him."

"He was the only person I had ever met until last week on the road."

"Which road?"

"The road that led here."

"From where?"

"From where I came."

"You met someone on the road?"

"Yes, merchants."

"Where were they going?"

"They were going to the place from which I had come."

"And where is that?"

"I don't know."

"This little girl can't help the rebellion," announced Astrahn. "Mentally, she's a spoffet-toed chowgis."

"I suppose you're right, Astrahn, but she's uncorrupted, she goes without the usurper's mark, and it is our duty to protect her."

"Protect me from *what*?" I asked.

In the instant before their answer we were shaken by a tremendous explosion. All changed. Everyone froze momentarily, overcome by fear. Then the music stopped and the skaters dropped to the ice and frantically began to unlace their skates. Lights started to go out, and from every direction came the sounds of running.

Suddenly a huge red fire began to burn in the sky above,

coloring the frozen city with the hue of blood. An immense flare lofted by a trench mortar now descended slowly under a parachute, swinging to and fro like a jailer's keys.

In red light so bright that it hurt my eyes, I saw everyone running. "What is it?" I asked.

"Don't you know?" Notorincus said as he and Astrahn struggled to gather up their baking tools. "How long have you been here?"

"I arrived at dusk today."

"It's curfew," Astrahn said. "The square must be clear in five minutes; in ten minutes, the first ring of the city; in fifteen, the second ring; and so on. Within half an hour all the rings of the city will be absolutely empty, so the usurper can ride through the streets at night in his chariot, clad in his black robes, and kill anyone he sees. And anywhere that he is not, his soldiers are, doing their best to imitate their master."

Even though Astrahn and Notorincus hurried and were about to break away, I asked, "What is the purpose of emptying the streets? Is it just so the usurper can ride through a dead city?"

"Control," said Astrahn. "Every night he must prove to himself that his power is absolute, and every night he does."

Though the usurper had killed my parents and grandparents, though I was only ten years of age, though he rode in a chariot and I was unarmed, and though he had killed long before I was born, even before my mother or father were born, I was not afraid. I cannot tell you why, but I simply was not afraid. They say now that it was in my blood, but I say that it was a gift from a kingdom far and clear.

"Where are you staying?" shouted Notorincus. "You must arrive there within three minutes!"

"I'm not staying anywhere," I said, calmly.

"Oh no!" they both shouted. "We can't take you in, because we already have seventeen. One more and the compartment will be so full they'll smother. You must find a hiding place."

"I'm not afraid of the usurper," I said.

They stopped dead, even as precious time was passing, even at risk to their lives, for they had never heard these words before.

From the far end of the palace square came the thunder of a phalanx of cavalry a mile wide. Though distant, they approached at a gallop.

"You may not be afraid," Notorincus cried as we began to run once again, "but if the usurper sees you he'll kill you. And if the soldiers catch you they'll bring you to selection. We bake in the palace, and we know secrets. Listen carefully. At selection, tell them that you're a yam curler."

"A what?" I asked, but they were swept away from me on tides of panic, and as I ran I remembered the words *yam curler* though I did not know what they meant. Nor did I know what Notorincus meant by selection.

The awful red light descended, and even as I sought the shadows I could feel its heat against my back. The cavalry came like a tidal wave, tramping down the snow until the square behind them glinted, until the surface was so smooth that wind-propelled remnants of timber and tent cloth were swept along like reeds blown across the ice.

In the forest we had had none of the entertainments common to cities, and if those we had were somewhat idiosyncratic, they were excellent preparation for life as it has unfolded. One of my games, for example, was to lie on the ice of a mountain lake until I could no longer feel the cold. Thus, as the evening passed, I was not uncomfortable in the frigid air.

Though I was unfamiliar with the social graces, and dancing, and what was in a zoo, a bakery, or a museum, on a clear day when I had neither lessons nor work I would run in the mountains sometimes from dawn until dark. In short order I would reach the state of perfect balance in which running up a mountain slope seemed to require no effort, running on the flat was like riding, and to run downhill was to fly.

Thus, as others had fled the palace square in gales of emphysema, I left as fast and easily as a mounted rider. Long before the start of curfew I had bounded to the Fifth Ring of the city, where all was quiet and everyone had gone to bed. The prosperous noblemen of the Fifth Ring did not, like everyone else, go to the palace square at night. Instead, they had early dinner parties and sat by their fires, on silken chairs, drinking whiskey and reading biographies of the usurper.

I knocked half-heartedly on a few doors, knowing that no one within would open them on a winter night after curfew. I imagined that at times other people too had been driven into the Fifth Ring, with soldiers trailing not far behind. And those who live in warmth on the far side of oaken doors usually have lost their taste for combat so long before and so completely that they do not even like to witness it, much less throw themselves to its mercies.

For a few moments I drifted about, admiring the lovely houses, the flawless iron fences, the iced-over brooks in serpentine parks with gilded bridges, and then I heard the distant sound of horses.

Not far up the street were some garbage bins, which I thought were for housing animals or storing grain. I went to the first one, opened it, and turned away, trying to keep my stomach down. In a city where it was fashionable to eat virtually anything, the garbage can had been stuffed with giraffe innards. The second was even worse, but then I saw another one overflowing with excelsior.

The cedar excelsior was as clean and fragrant as the other bins' contents had been nauseating. I lifted the top and burrowed in. It was warm and comfortable, and I yawned. It seemed a fit place to try to sleep, and I almost did fall asleep, but then a group of horses and riders rounded the corner. Feeling entirely invisible, I thought the best way to hide was simply to go limp. If I slept I would be calm, and they would go away.

I was awakened much later, when I was much colder, by voices and the sound of horseshoes against the cobbles.

"That's excelsior," said one of the voices. "They use it to wrap delicate objects. Because it's in front of the house of a nobleman, there might be something valuable in it, that the unpackers overlooked. Wolfgang, Bonticlaw, turn it over and pull out the packing."

I heard two men leap from their horses, and boots on the stone. I closed my eyes as I was turned upside down and rolled out into the night air on a breaking wave of excelsior.

Hands tied behind my back, I rode folded over the hindquarters of a horse. As we had ridden along the main radial of the Fifth Ring, we had joined a cavalry detachment of fifty. Some of the cavalrymen had captives, and some wore blood-spattered clothes. They were happy and proud, but I could hardly bear to look at them. I wondered if I had been right to come to this place, to leave behind the gentle life I had had in the mountains, when sometimes I would see the moon from my bed, voluminous and yellow, floating over distant snowfields.

Just before midnight—I could tell by the position of the very same moon, which now seemed cold and cruel—we had come through an industrial district in the Third Ring, where all you could hear was the roar of fires and the sound of metal striking metal. As we were about to cross a bridge over a canal, the commander of the detachment called a halt. So quickly did the horses stop that I was thrown against the chain mail of my captor and I watched some cavalrymen fall from their saddles.

"Back in!" came the cry all the way down the line. "Honor his coming!"

The horses sidled and kicked. The men pushed them and swore. But in less than a minute the troop had formed itself into rows on either side of the road. The horses were forced to their knees, the men went there as volunteers, and when the lines were completely straight the soldiers hung their heads as if in shame. Then I heard what the commander had heard earlier at the head of his troop—the sound of steel wheels rushing over roads and cobbles. The air was so disturbed that it moaned and shrieked as if with the clash of a hundred swords.

"All bow!" the commander screamed, and every soldier and most of the horses bent their heads. In the bright moonlight it seemed that fifty gleaming silver spheres had been put upon fifty supernatural bodies, and the light glinted off helmets and weapons like the spray of a waterfall dashing upon ice-encrusted rock.

As the usurper's chariot rattled over the bridge, the noise became deafening. No one was supposed to look at him, least of all someone like me, and the penalty for transgression was death. But, once, I had been miraculously spared, as had my mother, and I acted accordingly.

While the soldiers might see only a hoof or the lower part of a wheel, I saw him, I looked directly at his face, and I did not fear. He was tall and heavy, and his boots made him seem even taller as he stood on the platform of a chariot that thundered past as if we did not exist. His face was scarred and twisted, his towering form draped in black robes that flew in his wake like the wings of a crow that dies in midair and cartwheels to the ground. He wore a mask that made him look like death itself. The wind that followed him was cold, and his own soldiers feared him so much that they held their heads down until their chins pressed against their breastplates.

When I saw that he was real, I determined to dispatch him into the black world whence he had come. I have yet to kill him, and I collect armies now the way other people bring wood to the stove. Someday, he will come back, and I will have my chance. We rode on.

As one detachment joined another we became part of a great river of horses and men. I have seen such things a

thousand times since, and still they impress me. Then, it was new, I was a child and a captive, and I was amazed by the might and the force.

At a barracks near the palace square my hands were unlashed, I was removed from the horse, and they put me in a wooden wagon that held whole families—fathers, mothers, children, grandparents, and even dogs. As soon as the door was closed the light disappeared and the only way to know that the others were still present was to hear the mothers comforting their softly crying babies.

"Where are they taking us?" I asked the darkness, and no one answered. I asked again, and no one would break the silence. I was a child, and it was for the children's sake that I received no answer.

At dusk the next day the door slid open and we left the wagon in disarray. Half of us were sick and feverish already, though not I. Others, having had neither water nor food, moved almost as weakly as the sick. Our worst enemy, however, was neither sickness nor lack of food and water, but the cold.

We were in a snowy forest that dusk had colored gray. The pines were still and the spaces between them mysterious. To our left was a group of low buildings and to our right a factory with six chimneys from which issued six streams of dark smoke that came together in an angry coil and then split off on currents of wind to disappear forever among the clouds.

"Line up," we were told, and we did. We filed slowly into a building, and when at last I stepped inside, one of the soldiers simply picked me up and threw me across the room, where other children had also been thrown, and lay crying.

I was the first to be selected. An enormous soldier picked me up, immobilized my arms, and carried me to the man at the table.

I didn't like the look of him, and I didn't like the look on the soldiers' faces, but, still, I was unafraid.

"And what were you doing out in the Fifth Ring after curfew, dear?" asked the man at the table. Had it not been for Astrahn and Notorincus, I dare not imagine what might have happened to me, but I knew exactly what to say.

"Curling yams," I said. "I was on my way to a yam curling job. I'm a yam curler."

He was dumbstruck. Evidently, in removing one pleasure I had substituted another, and he didn't know quite what to do. He motioned with his pen, and I was hustled out a door to a little yard, and back into a wagon. I lay on the floor, and through a crack in the boards I could see people in the line, but only the part of them between knee and thigh. I saw shawls, and suitcases, and children of all sizes moving as slowly as a river until they were eaten by the dusk and I could no longer tell the difference between the color gray, the black of night, the feeling of cold, the smell of smoke, and my own dark sleep.

The next I knew, it was daylight. Shivering and filthy, I was removed from the wagon by a red-haired middle-aged woman in a white tunic and chef's hat. I had the feeling that, though I had no idea of what a yam might be, she did.

Snow fell all around us and salted the air between my face and hers. The sleeves of my coat were glazed with snowflakes that shone in the gray light of the sky. I was deep inside the palace itself, in the courtyard of the yam kitchens, where wagons came by the thousand to unload yams of many colors. This courtyard was so big that you would need a full minute to gallop a good horse along any one of its sides. The wagons came and went through four tunnels, and walls of lighted windows rose into the dim reaches of falling snow.

"This is the yam section of the starch kitchens," she said. "We are responsible for yam output. Other regions handle potatoes, rices, and crusts for meat pies. The crusts were a great gift that the old emperor took from the bakers and gave to the starch section, in the time when we had empty rooms and idle hands."

"All those sacks of yam flour are for the crusts of meat pies?" I asked, eyeing a loggia upon which lay a pile of ten-thousand flour sacks marked, "Flour, Yam, Type II: Destination—Crust Division, Meat Pie Sector."

"Those are for the luncheon in recognition of the slavish obedience of the Duke of Tookisheim. The Duke of Took-isheim's newspapers are the most adoring of the emperor. In one issue of the *Tookisheim Post* alone, the emperor and his wife were depicted as divine beings fourteen hundred times. It taxed the engravers even more than does the government."

"Isn't that disgusting?" I asked. "Isn't it vile that the Duke of Tookisheim is so contemptuous of the truth?"

"Ssshh!" she said, putting her finger to her lips. "Don't say the incorrect word."

"What incorrect word?"

"The word you said."

"Truth?"

"Ssshh! That word was abolished years ago. It got in the way. It hurt the Duke of Tookisheim's feelings, because when there was that other newspaper, they used the incorrect word to make war on the emperor and to make fun of the Duke of Tookisheim and his brilliant young son, Peanut. But the Duke of Tookisheim knew what to do. He drove that other newspaper into bolivian."

"Why didn't the emperor just close it down?"

"He let the Duke of Tookisheim and Peanut defeat it fairly and squarely, so no one could say he was a bad emperor. In the end, each issue of the *Tookisheim Post* weighed more than a horse. It had a section to suit everyone. We loved the yam articles in the starch section. And the Duke of Tookisheim's journalists were the best in the world at repeating things. The other newspaper might say *Ox*, but the Duke of Tookisheim's newspaper would say *No Ox! No Ox! No Ox! No Ox! No Ox! No Ox! No Ox! No Ox!*, again and again and again, until, even if an ox had been standing on your head you would be convinced that there was no ox, no ox, no ox, no ox, no . . . oh, excuse me."

"Ox," I said, thinking that this woman might have been more than what met the eye.

"Now, we *all* love the emperor. The emperor can do no wrong. The emperor is good. He is a genius. He loves us all. He will live forever. The old emperor was bad. The old emperor was selfish. You know, the emperor freed us from the old emperor."

"Yes, I know," I said. She was speaking of my grandfather.

"He slew him."

"I thought the old emperor died a natural death."

"Did he?" She laughed. "I don't know! I don't know!" she said cheerfully. "All I know is what the Duke of Tookisheim tells me!" She winked. It might have been frightening. There were many like her, but she was not what she appeared to be. Eventually I learned that she was a friend of Astrahn and Notorincus, and that she, too, had taken the oath of rebellion. But we were in the palace itself, where love of the new emperor was mandatory. And yet the only real love of the emperor came from the emperor himself, and other than that, all opinions were creatures of falsity and fear, even if not everyone knew, even if the Duke of Tookisheim's and Peanut's thorough repetitions had done their work of hypnosis.

"The bakeries are on our east wall," said Elena, the pretending admirer of the Duke of Tookisheim. "They are much bigger than the yam kitchens, of course. Well, naturally. And the chocolate kitchens are on the south wall. Though the chocolate kitchens have six thousand chefs and workers and we have only three thousand, they are divided by law into three sections—

beverages, candy, and desserts. So, really, we are bigger than they, especially as the dessert section of the chocolate kitchen is half under the jurisdiction of the bakers."

Here is where I chose to penetrate her veil. "Bakers?" I asked. "Would you happen to have made the acquaintance of one Astrahn and one Notorincus?"

She burst into an idiotic peal of soprano laughter and rushed to embrace me. But as I recoiled, she whispered, four octaves lower, "Shut up, my dear. People are listening. All in good time."

"You must tell me," I responded, dropping as many octaves as I could (because of my age I was still far to the right of the *Steinweg*), "what, in God's name, is a yam curler. What is a yam? I don't want to go back to selection."

"A yam, you see," she told me, "is the edible starchy tuberous root of the various plants of the genus *Dioscorea* (as in *D. Sativa*, or *D. Alata*) that largely replaces the potato as a staple food in tropical climates and is cooked in the same way but has coarser flesh."

"Oh."

"It is necessary for everyone in the yam kitchen to know that, lest he be accidentally sequestered to the yak kitchen."

"What is a yak?"

"A big animal, like a buffalo, but it looks less like a French poodle and more like a grass hut."

"What is a yam *curler?*"

"In time, my dear, you will wish that you had never heard the word."

Then she took me on a tour of the yam kitchens. Never having heard of a yam, I had had no way of knowing that it existed in several hundred varieties. A score of these were being prepared for the Duke of Tookisheim's lunch the next day, it being well known that Peanut was a big yam lover. Master carvers made of yams detailed representations of castles, angels, galleons, barges, and trees. I thought this was yam curling, and I swallowed hard, because I couldn't whittle.

Again the peals of soprano laughter. Again the conspiratorial drop in octaves, as we went from one huge yam hall to another. "A yam curler, my dear," she said as she glanced left and right to check for prying eyes, "does not carve. Curling a yam means standing on the yam sorting apron as the yams roll down, and sweeping the paths in front of them with a broom."

"That's all?"

"Don't underestimate it," she said. "You must know several hundred types of yams, their trajectories and destinations, their coefficients of friction and how they roll over the dust of all the other yams. The permutations are staggering. I hope you can calculate in your head."

I looked at her as if we both were crazy.

"The danger, too. The yam sorting apron has a variable slope. On humid days or before a royal lunch, it is slightly steepened. You can slip and roll into any one of dozens of choppers, peelers, cauldrons, ovens, or, God help you, into the yam disposal shaft, which falls two hundred feet into a pit simply seething with tremendous, horrendous, yam-eating—aahhs!" she said, unable to repeat the name of whatever it was that consumed the broken and imperfect yams.

"We'll get you set up," she told me. "Before ascending to your room, you can take a long hot bath in slightly yammish parboiling water, change into clean clothes, and have something to eat. Tonight the yam workers are having woodchuck pie with yam salad and yam pudding."

"Ascending to my room?"

"The dormitories are full, so I'm afraid you'll have to sleep in a little room in the tower. It's very cold there, but we managed to salvage—steal, actually—a new featherbed that was mistakenly delivered to the starch courtyard. It had been on its way to one of Peanut Tookisheim's sycophants, and is three feet thick. The stairs to the tower collapsed when the old emperor's astronomical telescope was smashed, so you'll have to ride up on a rope."

"Why was his telescope smashed?"

"The new emperor does not want us to look beyond what happens in his kingdom. He says it is wrong and useless. He hates the stars because he cannot ever hope to govern them, so they are now incorrect. Don't say the word in public. Don't admit to having looked into the night sky."

I bathed in a huge vat of only slightly yammish hot water, was given a yam curler's black velvet dress trimmed with orange silks, had a fulsome meal of woodchuck pie, and went to the tower, where Elena comforted me before my counterweighted ascent. The shaft above disappeared into its own length and darkness, but I was not afraid, as I had grown up in the mountains and frequently gone with the goats to places most little girls could not even dream of. It took ten minutes of steady rising to get to my chamber at the top, the very chamber in which I am now writing down my story for you.

I spun gently on the rope and passed window after window through which I could see swirling snow and a golden sun clothed in frozen light.

This little room as I first saw it was not what it is now, after royal artisans have filled the cracks, reglazed the windows, laid a new floor, and enameled the walls and moldings until, years after the paint was applied, it still looks wet. In those days it was perpetually cold as the wind shrieked through the cracks. The floor was rotten, the walls peeling, and every surface covered by spider webs and grime.

But I could still see through the windows high above the city, the lake, and the palace. I threw one open, and looked out on the palace side. As the bitter air flowed in and magnetized to the floor, what I saw was so astonishing that it became impossible to think of comfort. Horsemen and couriers who rode from place to place upon the palace roofs would head for the distance in any direction and soon pass from sight. So many chimneys spouted smoke that I felt like an Arctic captain surveying a patch of rigid emerald sea where all the whales of the world had gathered in a mighty fleet. Now and then, a figure would emerge from a door and step onto the roof to shake out a mop, release a pigeon, or take a breath of air. And the plain before me was so vast that these people would emerge every second or two, as if they were marking time on a clock. Closing the window, I sank exhausted to the featherbed and wrapped myself in its folds. Soon I was warm, and I began to fall in and out of sleep like a boat rocking on the tide. Before I was pulled into the gravityless world, I stroked my forehead, and closed my eyes as if my mother and father were kneeling by my bed. All children should have parents who love them as I will love you, but those who are born to be alone can be comforted only by an impossible task. My task was certainly not easy, and at every moment it brought to me the love that I had never known.

In the morning when I left my bed and put on my yam curler's dress I was so cold that an icicle could have formed on my back. I put my arms through the rope loop and stepped into the abyss. Slowly descending through blackened air and frozen smoke, I wondered how I could capture a kingdom so vast that the royal palace was divided into provinces and the button storage rooms employed six hundred clerks.

At tables twice the length of war galleons, in a room that was so big that sometimes a shooting star would flash in one of its corners or skid upon the horizon, the yam workers were eating stacks of dangerously hot yam cakes, with smoked wild boar sausage and the syrup of the North German Hippopotamus Yam, which is too sweet for baking and far too large to be a super-miniature yam, the kind that are glazed in chocolate and popped into the mouth ten at a time. So it is squeezed for its syrup in special silver presses that don't get sticky. These were in a room next to the gymnasium and evening club for the personnel of the yam research library and laboratories. I passed there once.

Breakfast was good. We brushed our teeth at long alabaster sinks with mango and pineapple motifs on the faucet handles, suggesting that once the yam kitchen had been attached to the realm of tropical fruit.

Then I was taken to the sorting apron. In the first few weeks I came quite close to death by boiling, chopping, frying, baking, or simply a plunge into the pit of yam-eating aahhs! Whatever they were, you could hear their squeaks echoing faintly up the 200-foot shaft. The apron was extremely slippery, and the slipperiness was not uniform. Different types of yam dust had different coefficients of friction. As you swept and cheered the yams toward the sorting gates, you could easily slip on your hip. Down you would go, sliding toward one of the deadly exits.

You had to right yourself immediately, and, if you could not, make your broom perpendicular to the shaft, and there you would dangle above the squeaks, hot oils, or automatic knives until you could crawl back to the apron.

At ten I was nimble and new enough to learn this very quickly, and soon I was doing my job effortlessly. This did not mean I was happy. Indeed, I was not. For my task was so daunting that I was haunted. Upon entering the city I had been overwhelmed by the complexity and power of the obstacles I would have to overcome were I to reach thc usurper. His power came not from within, for he himself was less than nothing: his power came from the webs of things that were spun around him.

What could I do? For one, I was not allowed anywhere but the sorting area of the yam kitchen. Were I to have appeared, for example, in the frying halls, my pass would have been wrong and I would have been sent to selection.

I doubted very much that the usurper even knew of the yam kitchens, much less the sorting area. He might not even have been aware of the starch section. And if ever he even took a bite of yam, he might have mistaken it for a sweet potato. That's how expendable we were, how isolated, and how unknown. I despaired after thinking of a hundred unworkable schemes—arming the yam workers and bursting through the kitchen barriers, descending from my tower onto the palace roofs and journeying through the ducts to assassinate the usurper; and others, all made impossible by the armies of guards and the guarding armies and the fact that no one I might ask knew where in the palace the royals actually lived. You could walk about for the rest of your life and not see half of it.

Not being able to do anything, I did nothing. Every day I felt as if I had sunk lower and lower, as if I had failed. As I resigned myself to my odd form of slavery, the darkness seemed impenetrable. Then came a friendly ray of light.

One bleak morning in January, long after I had been inured to growing old like Elena in the yam kitchens, she came to me at the sorting apron and called me down. She brought me over to a window, past which the snow flew in driving lines that suddenly would change course with a snap, like a dog shaking its prey.

"You've been taken from the sorting apron," she said, almost whispering, looking at me in a wondering way. "You are the first person ever to be removed from the apron before the normal passage of the five-year apprenticeship."

I had no idea what was happening.

"Perhaps you're a rhubarb spy . . ." she said, looking at me carefully.

"What is a rhubarb spy?" I asked.

"You're not a spy. But I don't understand. You've been instructed to move to the distant margins of the yam kitchen, to the sector near the door to the world of the bakeries. None of us has ever been there. You will be able to see through that door to the great avenues of ovens, and it is said that things happen there that we cannot even imagine."

"Why not just walk through the door and take a look?" I asked.

Elena jumped back as if I had hit her. "Child, you talk like a princess! No yam worker has ever passed into the bakery section and come back. You know not of what you speak, for the world is wider than you can conceive."

I shrugged my shoulders. Even before I had discovered who I was and whence I had come, the freedom of the mountains had taught me to believe that the world was, indeed, mine, that I was forever free, that only God could tell me my place.

"Through that door," Elena went on, "pass the yam syrups and honeys that the bakers use invisibly to give their breads and cakes a touch of art. We've been told that you are needed there to push the carts and load the pallets. Why you when we have men four times your size? How should I know? I only know what the Duke of Tookisheim tells me."

"The Duke of Tookisheim told you that?"

"Of course not. I would never be able to speak to a duke. I would never be privileged to speak to someone who had met someone who had spoken to a duke."

"Who told you then?"

"Ssshh! Don't hear. It was Astrahn and Notorincus."

"You do know them," I said. "How? They're bakers."

"Though yam workers are forbidden to trespass in the bakeries, bakers can enter the yam kitchens. They are like noblemen. And they told me. Now, go! If you're late they'll be angry."

"Astrahn and Notorincus wouldn't be angry at *me*," I said, somewhat royally.

"Young lady, Astrahn and Notorincus are our betters. You must not assume or instruct in their regard. Is that clear?"

"But Elena, Notorincus is a slave, and Astrahn is the slave of a slave. How can they be our betters?"

"Ah! You are so foolish! If you work hard all your life you may be lucky enough to become the slave of a slave. Even the slave of a slave cannot be taken to selection (unless he is caught with a watch on his person), and he can be killed only by a nobleman. We, on the other hand, well, it is assumed that we go to selection, and only our great good luck that we don't. No law says we don't. We have merely been overlooked, like a colony of insects in a beam lost deep within the palace. That is why you must hold your breath as you live, and it is why you must love the emperor and praise him, and be happy with whatever the Duke of Tookisheim tells you."

I nodded, but I turned to the window and under my breath I said, "When I get to be queen, I am going to have this duke brought before me on a *spit*, and I'll say, 'Tookisheim, I hope you have a strong heart, for you are going to make one turn over the fire for every lie that has ever been trumpeted from your fop-filled newsrooms.'"

I hadn't realized that I was no longer free, that I had to look up to the slave of a slave and bat my eyelashes like a little doll. I didn't like that. I really didn't like that, and I stomped through the yam kitchens with such anger and disgust that everyone stepped out of my way.

This usurper, who was not of royal blood, had taken my kingdom, and if I had had an immense angel with a sword behind me, as once I may have, I would have flown through the solid walls of the palace to slay him without further ado. But I had a longer road to travel than just that, and I soon found myself pushing carts of yam syrups to the door between the bakery world and the yam world in which I was trapped like a fly in a honey crock.

"Who is this little girl who is so surly?" one of the soldiers at the doorway asked as I stood, scowling, while the cart was unloaded on the other side before it was pushed back to us.

No one answered.

"I asked, who is she?" the soldier said, his hand migrating slowly to his sword.

All those around me were so terrified that they could not move. "Apologize to him," one of them whispered, "or our wives and children will be sent to selection."

Obviously, I had no choice. I dropped to one knee, bent my head, and said, "Majesty, please forgive one who is lower than the slave of a slave. I was not surly, I was speechless in awe of your greatness."

A moment passed, and the soldier smiled. "All right," he said. "I'll take only half the children to selection. The others may live."

In this moment time stood still. The mothers and fathers of the children who pushed the carts were both grateful and grieved. Their hearts broken yet again, they prepared to lose their children, and at the same time they were grateful that half would be spared.

But royal blood is royal blood. "This is a gift?" I asked, straightening, holding my head high. Even the soldier was amazed. "This is your smiling gift? That you will kill only half the children?"

I haven't the slightest idea of what I would have done next had not Astrahn and a group of slaves burst in from the bakery side. Astrahn pulled a short broadsword from within the folds of his slave tunic and killed the first soldier. Then two other soldiers drew their own swords and approached Astrahn rather contemptuously. I suppose they simply did not believe that a slave could fight, especially as odd-looking and buff-colored a creature as Astrahn. But that a slave could fight was, indeed, the last thing they ever learned.

A woman in the background began to shriek and wail that

we would all die, that everyone in the yam kitchens would be slaughtered.

I was going to give my speech then. And, who knows? It might have worked, and it might not have. Probably not. They were too afraid. They wouldn't have believed me when I told them who I was. But before my first words could tumble forth, Astrahn put his hand over my mouth and pulled me back. The other slaves quickly loaded the soldiers onto carts, covered them perfectly, and gave instructions to the trembling yam workers.

"You people have a shaft at the end of which are yam-eating . . . what do you call them?"

"*Aahh!*" was the horrified answer.

"Whatever. Drop these gentlemen in and wash the carts. Then go back and continue as if nothing has happened."

"What about the blood?" someone asked, but the bakery slaves were already scrubbing the floors.

"Everyone be silent," Astrahn commanded. He then said something that made my heart soar and filled my eyes with a picture of the future.

"You are now sworn to the rebellion. Whether or not you would have chosen it, it is now your path."

I myself could never be sworn to the rebellion, as the oath was pledged to the rightful sovereign, who was me.

From that moment on, everything proceeded at very high speed. I was whisked away, my badge was changed, and the next thing I knew I was traveling, with Astrahn and Notorincus on either side of me, high above a great plain of bakers and their ovens. I felt as if we were flying, but we were merely riding on a bench that had been suspended from one of the overhead conveyor chains that were used to carry supplies.

"Nice to see you again," Notorincus said, bashfully of course. "Would you like to take a nap?"

"A nap?" I asked. "What will happen next?" I feared that I wouldn't know what to do, and wanted them to brief me, as fast as they could, before we had to leave the aerial bench.

"It will take five or six hours to cross the bakery floor," Astrahn said in his somewhat elevated way. "Why don't you rest for a few hours, and then we'll tell you what you must do. Nice to get some rest, no?"

I fingered my new badge. Theirs were yellow with red borders, mine purple and gold.

"Yes," Astrahn said. "Ours are the highest-level bakery badges.

Yours is the highest-level service badge for the royal quarters, which are many hours away."

"Why?" I asked.

"Don't worry," Notorincus said. "Though it's forged, no one can tell the difference."

"But what am I going to do?"

"Have a rest, and when you've got your strength back, we'll tell you."

As I leaned against Notorincus, I was warmed by his soft and furry pelt, and we climbed a little on the chains, always speeding forward gently. Under the roof ahead was darkness, and in the limitless open space below, the fires of a hundred thousand ovens were twinkling in the distance. Far beneath us, bakers in their remote islands and avenues moved calmly, baking and glazing, writing whole books with their pastry tubes. They didn't know that we were gliding high above them in the warm air that smelled of cakes and icing. The chain made a pleasant, old-fashioned, clinking noise, and Notorincus patted my head. "Take a nap," he said. "Have a good sleep. We'll awaken you an hour or two before we approach the bakery frontier. All will be well."

My eyes could hardly believe the gentle scene before me, or that such a roof could exist without a single column, but then

I remembered that the sky, which was far greater, had not a single column either.

"Sleep," said Notorincus, and as we calmly sailed through the darkness, I did.

When I awoke I thought I was dreaming. We had risen to such a high altitude that no longer could we see the individual bakers at work on the plain below, and the fires of their ovens looked like a carpet of gold stars. The air was clear and the roof above us invisibly black. Other than a faint rush of warm wind and the occasional muted sound from the apparatus that carried us along, all was silence.

"You're up," Notorincus said.

I rubbed my eyes and yawned.

"You had a good rest. You slept for four and a half hours and you didn't stir once: your sleep was deep."

"Is it night or day?"

"We don't know. Near the frontier there are no windows to the outside, and we haven't passed a courtyard in an hour."

"Don't you have a watch?" I asked.

"Bakers use hourglasses, and if a slave is caught with a watch he is sent to selection. But Astrahn risks all. He has a watch."

"The slave of a slave has a watch?" I asked.

"I was not always the slave of a slave," Astrahn said, with such great dignity that I felt ashamed for my question.

"Before I fell into slavery I was a general of the Damavand cavalry. After the usurper murdered the Prince of Esterhazy, we continued to serve the good emperor, but we knew the day would come when the usurper would take his place, so we prepared for war.

"The good emperor's son took the throne, but the usurper remained. Only when the son was murdered did the Damavand rise. Given the enormity of the crime, how could we not have risen?"

I choked, prepared to hold back tears.

"Somehow the good emperor's son had discovered the daughter of the Esterhazys, grown to womanhood. This was a miracle, for we all had believed that she had been killed with her mother and father. But then the usurper found them, and their child, and finished the task he had started so long before. Not only did he murder the prince and the daughter of the Esterhazys, but their newborn infant, who would have been our queen.

71

"Three generations of our royalty have fallen to him, and the blood of those generations is our blood."

"Do you know anything," I asked, "about the infant princess?"

"There is a legend," he answered, "that, like her mother, she escaped. There is a legend," he said, "that she lives. It is said, or it once was, that an angel stood behind her, that she was saved, and that when she returns, a fiery angel will announce her coming. If it were so, the people would rise up all at once, a great weight would be lifted, and the light of our days would come clear. But I fear that it is not so. Ten years have passed."

"And if she did return," I asked, "and the people did rise, would they be slaughtered?"

Astrahn smiled at me bitterly and wearily. He was, after all, a warrior who had become a slave. And he had sworn to conduct a rebellion that, after ten years, must have seemed impossible. How brave he was. "If she returned," he said, with his voice full of an emotion I could not then understand, "if she returned, a hundred Damavand generals would emerge from slavery and armies would form around them like swarms of bees. The announcement that she lives would spread like lightning, and no one would sleep until the armies were gathered to strike at the usurper. But we must find another way, or be forever lost in a dream."

"What is the other way?"

"I am not high enough to know. All I can tell you is that you have been summoned to appear at a dinner for the Legates of Pomerania and the Viscounts Regent of Dolomitia-Swift."

"Summoned by whom?"

"We down here know not by whom."

"But you are a general."

"Ah, but as there are slaves of slaves, there are generals of generals."

"What am I to do at this dinner? Who will be there? Where will it take place?"

"It is a state dinner in one of the petite dining rooms: only a thousand guests will attend, but it's very important. The usurper must throw the most exquisite dinner for the viscounts, because Dolomitia-Swift is the only kingdom that is more powerful than our own. The royals, the guests of honor, and the usurper himself will sit upon the water dais, where you will refresh flowers between courses. They use small girls for this, for you must walk along tight paths on the table to place the roses and peonies. When boys do it they kick over the stemware and the usurper selects them right on the spot. He'll select you too if you do the same, but girls are more graceful. Just be careful."

"The usurper eats?"

"Yes, at a table of fifty upon the water dais, which floats in a crystal pool over the sides of which water flows in a continuous and even fall that is lighted from within. Those who dine upon it think they are as high as the angels. And there you will be, walking delicately upon a vast table, carrying blooms to the flower stations."

I tightened my lips, and asked, "Am I to kill the usurper?"

"No!" Astrahn cried, while Notorincus shook his head to and fro like a dog shaking off water, saying "No! No! No! No!"

"Why not?" I asked.

"First of all," Astrahn said, "how would you do it?"

"I don't know. I'd hit him."

"Don't be ridiculous. He wouldn't even know you were there. And even were you able to kill him it would do us no good, as we have no sovereign. A rebellion must feed upon the hope not only of pulling down one flag, but of raising another in its place.

"And, then, it may be that *no one* can kill the usurper."

I looked at him askance.

"The usurper isn't a simple soldier, and all precautions have been taken to protect him. His cloak is of a secret metal fiber that is so light it floats and so strong that it sloughs off the bolts of the heaviest crossbow. His mask is of the same stuff, and he always wears a hat."

"His throat?"

"Protected by the cloak. He may look horrid, but he's safe. The only way to wound him would be to strike his cheeks, and this has been tried, as you will understand when you see the many scars there, but it has never sufficed to kill him."

"Astrahn, why am I being brought there?"

"Quite frankly, my dear," Astrahn replied, "I don't know. You'll have to see."

He peered ahead, and pulled a pocket watch from the folds of his tunic. It was a very beautiful, ornate, gold disk set with lighted jewels.

"How do the jewels glow?" I asked.

"Within is a tiny fire that will burn as long as it is not questioned. If you doubt it, it goes out."

"Who would doubt it?" I asked. "You can see its light with your eyes."

"There are some," Astrahn replied, "who are so pinched and checkered of soul that they stare upon it and doubt it still. Now, let's see." He held the watch away from him, as an aged person might, and read the time. "Six-twenty. The problem is, I never know if it's a.m. or p.m. I think it's evening now, and I think we should soon be coming to the frontier."

Within a minute or two of Astrahn's pronouncement we began to descend, gliding lower and lower through the darkness toward a great jewelled cliff, where the door was particularly busy with long trains of baked goods passing through, and the rest of the jewels were lighted windows in the wall of the royal reception sections. Some were like yellow sapphires, with candlelight showing through: others, dimly skylit, were like sapphires of blue. The small dining room was another hour's travel beyond the frontier, but I had begun to be nervous even before we left the conveyor. After all, I had never walked primly among stemware on a banquet table as big as a meadow.

Notorincus, who must have read my mind, said, "Don't worry, the flower girls are so good they have never kicked over a single glass. You'll see. Their skill and confidence will pass to you."

"How?"

"The music makes them certain, and encloses their every move within the golden rails of perfection. In fact, they seem to take pride in the danger, and to know that their flawless performance is a message of defiance.

"And they never fail, for if they fail, they die. There is a legend, on the flower-growing prairies of the southern roofs, that angels guide their feet."

We had come to the jewelled wall, and behind us stretched the vast darkness of the baking plain. I took a breath, and prepared to start my new career.

Leaving Astrahn and Notorincus behind, I journeyed for another hour to the heart of the royal reception region. I passed through so many an ornate chamber, so many a marbled hall, and so many a long gallery the end of which was far from sight, that I thought I might never return. In this journey I was escorted by two guides of the key, a class of people whose entire lives were spent studying the geography of the palace. All the guides of the key in the royal regions were old and crotchety, for they had been pulled in from the outer realms, where the disturbances were too great and the going sometimes too strenuous for any but the strongest youth.

"Where are we now?" I might ask.

"This is a secondary transit hall—see (they would say, pointing up), the gilding has relatively few angels—laid crosswise over the topmost tier of the Sixteenth Royal Desk Accessory Storage Structure. Structures fifteen through eighteen are for desktop items of ebony, burled walnut, alabaster, and amber. Unlike the gold, platinum, and precious stone structures, they need only rudimentary guard quarters and chapels, so the transit hall was run across the top."

"How close are we to the roof, then, if we are over the topmost tier?"

They laughed. "The roof, little yam slave with a royal pass, is *six hundred tiers above us*!"

I wanted to know what lay in those six hundred tiers.

"Would you really like us to say?" they asked, wrinkling their deathly pale faces so that their red eyes seemed to be set impossibly far back from their bladed noses. "We can tell you what is on every single tier. Shall we recite?" Powder flew from their wigs as a door ahead was opened, and their eyes flashed with sparks of vermilion light.

"No," I said, carefully. "Just tell me what is on the two hundred and twenty-eighth tier up, and the five hundred and ninety-third."

"Section four B," one said mechanically (they were totally insane), "subsection twelve, pillar seventeen, tier two hundred and twenty-eight: ladies underwear, archaic and out of fashion, silk. Tier five hundred and ninety-three: tomato fertilizer sticks, nontoxic, various lengths and thicknesses, for greenhouse use only."

Wanting to test their acuity, I asked, "Where might I find the tailor shop for the repair and maintenance of the winter clothing that used to be used by the podiatrists who were attached to the rhinoceros-horn carving apprenticeship program?"

"The African, the Asian, or the Mexican rhinoceros?" one of the key guides asked in the most disdainful way.

"Mexican rhinoceros?" was my reply. I thought I had caught them.

"Little yam slave," said the one whose wig had shed the most powder, his contempt so acidic that it burned through his teeth and tongue and twisted his face into what looked like an ancient bas-relief of a ram, "we have breeding programs: husbandry section five zero six, Seventeenth Agriculture Pavilion, fifteenth tier, Experimental Farming Tower, SW ten-forty."

"You idiots," I said. "You know everything but you know nothing. I ought to have you flayed alive for your preposterous arrogance."

This made them laugh. "Quite uppity for a girl yam slave," they twitted. "Do you realize," they continued, fingers dancing like the crazed tubes of an overstimulated sea anemone, "that either one of us, being true slaves, could have you selected for no reason whatsoever? We've passed a hundred security stations already, and as we get closer to the center they get thicker and thicker. All we have to do is bring you to one and point."

I said nothing, but a little while later the air grew so sweet that I knew we were near the honey vats. And when we raced along a catwalk above a lake of waxen honey, the kind used in royal chocolates, I urged them to peer over the rail.

"Why?" they asked.

"To see a special substructure in the honey vats that no key guide knows, but that even non-slaves in the yam kitchen sing of in their lullabies."

"That's impossible! The honey vats have no substructures.

The plum cordial vats have twenty-eight substructures, but that is due to the low viscosity of plum liqueur. The honey vats were built for an average viscosity of seven point two. They have no substructures."

"Right down there," I said. "I see them."

They leaned over to look, and as they did I bent, grasped an ankle of each one, and quickly stood up. Their hairpin legs became the levers that catapulted them over the rails. I watched them spin and tumble, and after they landed in the honey they shook their fists in rage, but I heard nothing of what they said, because they were too distant. They had quite a long swim ahead of them, as even the best swimmers cannot move through honey with prodigious speed.

I was lost, but I didn't feel lost, and I kept walking, taking turns here and there where I thought it might be appropriate. I felt as if, truly, the palace were mine and I had been in it many times before. I think this was my father speaking through my blood. He has done this so many times since, and he had done it, even without my knowledge, so many times before, that I am sure of it.

Though I never knew my father, his early touch taught me to rule, and though I took my mother's milk only for a short time, she has breathed into my lungs the clouds that float above the Damavand highlands, and the songs of the Veil of Snows. To them I owe all, and this I knew even then.

In crisp order I pre-positioned myself at the door of the flower girls, off the service ramp that led in a shell-like spiral up to the center of the water dais. I adjusted my yam curling dress, cleared my throat, and knocked.

The old man who received me was the flower master of the royal table, a Damavand to his toes. I announced that I had come from the yam kitchens.

"How did you get here without a key guide?" he asked in astonishment.

"I knew the way."

He looked at me as if to look through me, and then shook his head. Ignoring the thought that probably had shot through him like the momentary light of a distant summer storm, he said, "You were assigned key guides at the frontier. What happened to them?"

"Well," I said, "If in their curriculum the key guides do not give short shrift to swimming, they will eventually resume their profession. Otherwise, at some time in the far future when the honey vats are excavated for renovation two key guides will be memorialized in one of the many palace museums, perhaps next to dinosaurs in blobs of amber."

"Ah," he said. "You came *that* way." I don't think he knew what to make of me, as I had begun to speak with a pronounced royal twist.

"Yes," I answered. "And, by the way, I think that in the future I will decree that a middle light be placed between the red and green lanterns of traffic signals. It will be amber, to warn of one's fate if one ignores the change from green to red."

The flower master narrowed his eyes. "You are a crazy little girl," he said. "You talk like a queen." He looked about to see if we were within anyone's earshot. "Your badge is forged, and it can be detected. Don't call attention to yourself by talking like royalty. I don't know why, but the high generals summoned you here, and in less than half an hour you'll begin to refresh the flowers at the royal table as the banquet begins.

"Let me take you to the flower girls. They'll show you, on a mock-up of the table, exactly how to place bunches of peonies in the flower station between the Duke of Tookisheim and the Second Viscount of Dolomitia-Swift.

"Be careful. Your life depends upon it." And then, though not to me or to anyone in particular, he said, "I do not understand the high command. I simply do not understand them."

I was shocked to find myself suddenly among the flower girls, whose dress and footwear was more splendid than anything I had ever seen, and they were more amazed than I when I took to those clothes as easily as if I had been born in them. And though I was neither the oldest nor the tallest, I seemed to tower over the others. I exchanged my yam curler's dress for a blue silk that was achingly beautiful even in comparison with the other flower girls' rather splendid wardrobe. It had been provided for me, I was told, but no one knew by whom. I began to suspect that the Damavand generals in slavery had gotten wind of my presence. How else to explain the provision of this truly royal dress, and my sudden assumption from the yam kitchens to the water dais? I was wrong. The Damavand generals hadn't a clue that I was in the city or even that I was alive. But things seemed to be moving, if only by magic, and I did not want to stand in the way of my good luck.

As we waited, we gossiped, although I had nothing to gossip

about and knew none of the noble names that were flipped through the air like darts. I had taken my instruction from a little girl who, despite her absolute surety of foot, stuttered like an off-center mill wheel. I went over her directions again and again, not only to be sure of them, but because she spoke in multiple copies.

Pay no attention to the nobles. Ignore their conversation, which is idiotic, and listen only to the music. The music will make you feel as if the table is your garden and you are a princess happily taking flowers from it in bright sunshine. Walk gracefully, proudly, as if you were a noble yourself, as if the world were perfect.

At eight exactly, by the high-precision cuckoo clock in the hall where we waited, the music began. It would take half an hour for the nobles to assume their places, and then an equal amount of time for the royals to make their entrances and mount the water dais. Only after all were assembled would the usurper and his rock-cold queen ascend to their thrones at table, amidst cheers and applause from the nobles they fed, like dogs, with bits of gold and snippets of position. I vowed that when and if I became queen I would never indulge in such ritual, and I have not.

Though agitated, I was not afraid, and even had I been, the music would have given me courage, for music is the magical organizer of chaos, its presence a sure reminder that even the blackest darkness rests upon sparkling trusses of pure light, and by the time the usurper had been seated and the serving begun, I was ready to fly into any kind of battle and meet any kind of test. Then we were signaled by the flower master, and with our arms full of flowers we climbed the spiral stairs that led to an opening in the forest centerpiece, and we spilled out along our assigned pathways on the linen.

Laden with peonies, I walked slowly toward my station between the Second Viscount of Dolomitia-Swift and the Duke of Tookisheim. I curtsied, and fixed my gaze upon the blooms that were already there, waiting for one to wilt. Though my obligation was to keep my eyes riveted upon the flowers, this was my palace, my hall, and my table, so I looked about as I pleased. No one noticed. They were too absorbed in the music, their own conversation, and the dangers of placing a huge set of nobleman's buttocks upon a small velvet chair (had these chairs been of appropriate size, it would have been insulting). The dinner guests had arrived in upper-body masks, giraffe heads, cockatoo coats, and other oddities that, after their entrance, most entrusted to a mask-check girl. Others did not. Why do the very rich love to dress as birds, stingrays, Mandarins,

giraffes, pirates, and Nubian dancers? Can it be genetic? I have never found it anything but horrifying, and I have half a mind to abolish it.

I did not see the usurper at first, for though this was my hall, my table, and my palace, and though I had seen him before, I was hesitant to look closely upon the face of this man who had taken so much from me, my kingdom being the smallest part of it. When, in moving my eyes ever so cautiously, I locked them upon his repellent form, I saw there the marriage of power and evil.

Do not dismiss those who stand above you, for very seldom are they there by chance. Most often their power is genuine, their evil a power in itself, and their visage impressive. The usurper's face was many times the size of mine, and seemed even larger than it was. His smile was fixed, revealing huge teeth and immense incisors. He looked as if he might eat you, like a wild animal, and the plains of his cheeks resembled a battle helmet. Upon these plains were the scars of crossbow bolts, arrows, and knives, their presence a testament to his invulnerability.

You could see in his eyes that, if indeed he had a soul, it was someplace else, but that he was enjoying the dinner nonetheless, even if he enjoyed it not at all. He lived for absolute power, and his possession of it was confirmed in ceremony after ceremony, dinner after dinner, by the strength of his armies and the slavish obedience of his flacks. I had seen the selections. My own family had been among the first. This and my destiny kept me the model of girlish grace, smiling and light on my feet as I held my post. I turned my eyes from the usurper, determined to meet them one day, close and clear, in the presence of death. And from this I took a certain joy.

With no flowers wilting and nothing for me to do, I was able to turn my attention to the conversation. The Duke of Tookisheim, a snakelike cross between a ninny and a fop, was hectoring Peanut, who sat next to him in a raspberry-colored coat. The Duke totally ignored the Viscount of Dolomitia-Swift on his other side, because he was, apparently, incensed at Peanut's coiffure.

"Peanut, where did you have your hair done?" he asked.

"I didn't. I just took a shower and combed it out. Or, rather, I had a Pretzelian slave boy comb it out."

"How many times have I told you," the Duke said, "that Tookisheims take care of their hair? Look at mine. Do you know how many hours a day I spend on it?"

"I'm the one who runs the papers," Peanut said, holding a spoon like a knife pointed at his father, "and I didn't have time. Besides, my hair's different from yours. It's black. It already has gray in it. I have mother's hair. I prefer it. All your flounces make you look like a twit."

"You'll hear from me, Peanut!" the Duke of Tookisheim said. "You'll hear from me!" He was vibrating with rage, and all this was said in front of me, as if I were a statue, and would neither hear nor remember.

When the Duke was finished with Peanut, he produced a blizzard of compliments aimed at the usurper, and then, as his sycophancy grew flat he changed the tone to one of frustrated commiseration. "Sire," he said, "your reforms make much sense, but the people are selfish and their resistance maddening."

"The people need to be shown what is good for them, Tookisheim," the usurper said in a voice so deep that the stemware rattled.

"Yes, sire. You are a brilliant leader, and capable of convincing anyone of virtually anything, but the people are hoodwinked by the selfish Damavand generals hidden among the slaves. They spread the doctrine of self-interest, and they lie with impunity."

"And they must be destroyed," the usurper said, going into a funk.

"Come now, Tookisheim, old chap," said the Second Viscount of Dolomitia-Swift, in a voice that froze me in shock, "is it really so selfish for a person to attend to his own interests? Isn't that the stated purpose of the reforms, to serve all these people whom you call selfish?"

"Ah," said Tookisheim. "The point is, Viscount my boy, that laborers, petty merchants, and small farmers can't know what serves them best. They're always deluded and greedy. They think that if they are happy, all are happy, and they do not know that only if all are happy can they be happy. My task is to educate them, to lift them beyond their selfishness, to show them that each and every one of them must be willing to sacrifice himself for the good of all of them."

"But Tookisheim, old chap," the Second Viscount said, "consider the case of the paper makers of the Hoggenstrasse. They are taxed to death solely that they may enjoy the benefit of things such as the royal amputation wagons and compulsory tattoos. They don't want these things, and would be happier deciding how to use the fruits of their labor without interference. After all, you do."

"Yes," said Tookisheim. "But I'm *educated*. I don't live in a tiny little house. I don't lust after cheap bicycles and funny-looking clothes. What is the purpose of the elite if not to correct the misguided?"

"You may not lust after cheap bicycles, Tookisheim old chap, but you *are* covered in flounces, you have ribbons on your shoes, and you have enclosed your bulk in a sickening swamp-green coat."

"Naturally," the Duke of Tookisheim said, forgetting that he had checked his mask. "I'm a giraffe."

"Ah, but Tookisheim, a giraffe's brain is so much bigger."

"I beg your pardon!" said the Duke of Tookisheim. "How is it, anyway, that you presume to comment on the affairs of the kingdom, having arrived only this morning from Dolomitia-Swift, a place known to be strictly *bourgeois*."

"Don't be offended, old fellow," the Second Viscount of Dolomitia-Swift said with a cheerfulness that made the usurper boil. "Because we in Dolomitia-Swift desire friendly relations, we have made a careful study of your kingdom. Much is lacking, Tookisheim dear chap, and the heart of it is that you cannot rule in the name of your people if you imagine that it is your place to instruct them. You see, Tookisheim old fellow, in Dolomitia-Swift we learned long ago that when the power of government is married with the urge to instruct, it produces the bastard of coercion. And it doesn't matter what your motives are."

"This has gone beyond the bounds!" the usurper said, and,

upon hearing his voice, a thousand people moved to the edges of their little velvet seats. Even the waiters, usually models of discretion, stood pop eyed and open mouthed, their trays of caviar-stuffed road hen stilled in air. "I remind the Second Viscount of Dolomitia-Swift," the usurper growled in a tone so low that it was undoubtedly memorialized by the palace seismographs, "that my armies are overflowing with vigor and wanting of activity."

To this the Second Viscount responded, "Well said, Emperor. I receive your comments with all humility, and will be sure to repeat them to the generals of Dolomitia-Swift, whose armies, as you know, are, have always been, and will always remain . . . *invincible.*"

This galled the usurper, who knew that, in fact, the armies of Dolomitia-Swift were preternaturally invincible. Here the Duke of Tookisheim saw an opening, yet another opportunity to serve the usurper. "Why don't you shut up, you fat thing!" he shouted at the viscount.

The viscount laughed, and although I had not surely known him by his voice, I did know him by his laugh, and I trembled with joy that he had broken his vow. "Tookisheim, dear fellow," the viscount said, "I'm not fat. You are the one who is fat." And indeed, Tookisheim was whalish, elephantine, and porcine, although not necessarily in that order, whereas, even at an advanced age, the viscount was still trim.

"I'm going to have a section of the *Tookisheim Post* on how bad it is to make fun of fat people!" the Duke of Tookisheim shouted, shaking his finger at the viscount. "I'll have ten sections! And every day I'll have eight or nine articles— interviews with fat people whose feelings have been hurt, fat people who can't be in the Olympics, experts who tell us why we are so cruel, and why it's bad to be thin. I'll invent a new name for fat people. I'll call them hefty. I'll call them chunky. I'll call them beefy. No, I'll call them . . . muscular!" At this, the table exploded in laughter—even the usurper. And when the Duke of Tookisheim saw the usurper laughing at him, he laughed at himself, and was happy.

During this distraction, the viscount leaned forward and whispered to me. "My Queen," he said. "My dear Queen. How glad I am to see you, and thanks be to God that you are safe." And then, just before attention had begun to shift back to him, he quickly said, "Climb to the great clock before sunrise. You will find me in its workings."

This Viscount of Dolomitia-Swift was the man I had known since birth, he who had raised me as a daughter, who had taught me everything I knew. I was overjoyed to see him, but, as he had instructed me so long before, I could not reveal myself, and I had to hold back my tears. He had brought home all the long and sad history of the kingdom and broken my heart a dozen ways when he had addressed me as he did, for never before had he called me anything but *child*, or *daughter*, and, once again, with but two words, he had sung the song of my life.

I was so happy to see the tutor that I was not paying sufficient attention, and with my right foot I knocked over the Duke of Tookisheim's seltzer glass. The seltzer shot onto his plate and picked up a lot of beet juice, which then traveled with it in wonderful deflection until it stopped in the Duke of Tookisheim's face and fizzed down his cravat. The Duke of Tookisheim was now beet-colored in rage, or perhaps not in rage. Red bubbles made his eyebrows supernatural, and in any case he couldn't talk.

No one laughed. Except me. I laughed. After all, it was funny, and I was the queen. I admit that my royal demeanor was inappropriate to my situation, but it was so strong within me that I was unable to suppress it. My laughter was the only sound in the dining room, where you could have heard a flea dropping its diaper pin. And then, in the silence that followed, that flea's breathing would have sounded like the roar of the falls that plummet from the slopes of Mount Dalkash.

The usurper lifted his finger and motioned for me to approach. Though no one else was breathing, I was not afraid. I no longer knew how to be afraid, for I was the queen, and I trusted in my divine right.

I looked this man in the eyes, this man who had killed my mother and father, and I broke him. No one in attendance understood what had happened, not even he, not even I. But now I know. He could have killed me instantly in any of a hundred ways, and the witnesses would not have moved a muscle or even spoken of it after dinner. I was at his mercy. I had no power. I had no armies. I had nothing. But I was in the right, and I did not flinch.

Nor, might I add, did he. We stared eye to eye. "What," he

asked, in his booming voice—ah, the exhalations of pure fear that filled the hall!—"is so funny?"

I answered, like a queen, directly. "The Duke of Tookisheim has beet juice all over him, and he looks like an idiot. That's because he is an idiot."

At once Peanut Tookisheim jumped up. "My father is not an idiot!" he shouted.

"Shut up!" the usurper bellowed, the ice of his soul already beginning to shatter.

"Shut up!" Peanut Tookisheim said to himself, and sat down.

"You," the usurper said, pointing his finger at me from a clenched fist. "You . . ." It seemed very likely that he was going to kill me. What held him back was that I was tranquil, embraced by the bonds of providence.

In a defiant whisper, I asked, "What about me?"

How I tempted fate in those days when I was young. The usurper was about to dispatch me when the Second Viscount of Dolomitia-Swift rose from his seat and fearlessly, almost casually, addressed him in front of all. "As the child has been in my service at this meal, it will be an intolerable affront to my honor if she is harmed. Nay, if she is *inconvenienced*. The invincible armies of Dolomitia-Swift will strike your kingdom like a steel hammer upon eggshell. A diplomat must be treated with proper respect. It is the law of nations, and Dolomitia-Swift stands at the ready right now to prove my words. The decision, Emperor, is yours."

Of course, that was not so, as the real legate of Dolomitia-Swift was at that moment semi-imprisoned, playing an infinite number of backgammon games with Notorincus, who never won. Nonetheless, all was at stake, and a clock high on the wall ticked like a heart out of control. After much thought, the usurper turned to Peanut Tookisheim.

"Peanut Tookisheim!" he shouted. "You will receive fifty lashes, in public, on Saturday next, and everyone in the kingdom will rejoice. Not least I."

"What for, Majesty?" asked Peanut.

"For being a nitwit," the usurper growled.

In this instant I was whisked away by the flower master with such speed that I felt like a mail sack pulled into a speeding train. All the flower girls were running as fast as they could, and in the incredible panic in the halls underneath the water dais the flower master and I passed them. "You must hide for the rest of your life in the deepest recesses of the kingdom," he said.

"Not quite yet," I announced. "I have an appointment."

I can see the clock tower at this very moment, in the distance over the snow-covered roofs, standing higher than any building in the city. On this bright morning with a sky as blue as the ocean, it is crowned with white, and the winds aloft are playing with the snow upon its gables and cornices just as they do on the breathless ledges of the highest mountains.

After I had slipped through the bars at the base, I climbed in the cold and darkness up its many flights of stone steps. The windows gave out upon miasmas of ice and frozen fog, and if I reached to steady myself when rounding a turn I would quickly have to pull my hand from the stone lest the two be joined by cold. With every exhausting step in the freezing darkness I found a portion of despair, for it seemed that no matter how far I had come the kingdom was too massive to go any but the way of someone like the usurper.

Yes, the tutor had arrived, and he had worked his magic, bringing me from the depths to the heights, but what did this have to do with justice or vengeance? As long as the usurper had left the hall to cheers and I was obliged to hide, the tutor's wit and magic would be of no avail.

Still, I kept rising in the tower, wanting to see him, pushing the darkness ahead of me like a boat plowing through the night sea. It was my obligation and my desire, and eventually I came to the top of the stairs, where I turned the handle of a great door and it glided open in complete silence.

There before me, after all the darkness I had come through, was the kingdom's most wonderful room. I stepped in, closed the door, removed my heavy coat, and stood for a moment, forgetting why I had come, overwhelmed by pure observation.

I was as high above the ground as if I had been flying, as elevated as if on a summit in the first line of mountains, and yet I was in a vast room at the base of thirty stories of gleaming machinery that turned the hands of the four clock faces.

That which was not brass was gold; that not nickel, silver; that not glass, diamond or sapphire. The motive power for this machine, as the tutor had explained in what now seemed like the world before the world, was most extraordinary. A circular chain of platinum rods was draped over a geared wheel, all of gold, the size of a barn. Where the links of the chain were joined, a huge jewel the size of a melon was held in a mount. When the light of an electric arc pulsed through a battery of gems above and struck the jewels on the chain, the chain moved. The sequence had to be correct—sapphire to sapphire, diamond to diamond, emerald to emerald, and so on— but each burst of light pushed the jewels of the chain in a waterwheel of light.

As it moved, it generated the electricity that turned it, with much power left over. This, the tutor had said, was a perpetual motion machine, which, it was widely believed, could not exist. "But," he told me, and I remember this as if it were ten minutes ago, "the whole universe is a perpetual motion machine, which is to say that the original push was inexplicable except as evidence of divine splendor. So, if the entire universe is one of these machines that supposedly cannot exist, and we are in fact living inside it, why not have another?"

"Because only God is capable of building it," I answered, "not man."

"Right," the tutor said. "That we ourselves cannot build it goes without saying. That He can build it also goes without saying. It's all very simple. Yes?"

"Yes."

"Well, when we wanted another one, we asked for it."

"You did?"

"It took someone far wiser than I, but it worked."

"You mean, you asked God for a perpetual motion machine to power the clock, and it just appeared?"

"He sent it. At first He put it in the wrong place, but we revised our request and He moved it to the top of the tower."

I had never heard of such a thing, and I told him so.

"Why is it so hard to believe?" he asked. "He set up the universe, the sun, the galaxies, physical laws, and all that. Why not a clock?"

"That's wonderful," I said.

"I know," the tutor had answered.

There I stood, in a room that needed no guards, where human passion was modulated as if by magic, where the air was perfect, and the light sublime. I asked myself, who am I? A yam slave (not even a true slave), or the queen of the kingdom? And in this room the answer was absolutely clear that I was both, and that they were the same. And I asked myself, am I ten years of age or a newborn child or an old woman soon to die? And in this room the answer was the same. I was all, and none was different, not in this room. And I asked myself, can I feel pain? And the answer was, no, not in this room.

I thought of the child beneath her dying mother and father, and I thought of the child spirited across the mountains after her mother and father had sacrificed themselves so that she might live, and these thoughts that at most times I could not bear I was able to bear quite easily, in this room, for here all connections came clear, there was no longing, there was no lack. In this room perfection drove the clockwork, and its spilling over, its wonderful excess, like water tumbling over a weir, like the blast of sunlight at dawn, made everything come right. It was here that I understood that I need not grieve for those who are lost, for here I joined them.

As I walked amid the sometimes surprising flashes and sparkles of light in every color, and as the wheels turned and the darkness above sang with the progress of golden escapements, I remembered why I had come. "Tutor!" I called out. "Tutor!"

In this immense and perfect room, where would he be? I stopped to think, and the answer came. He would be in a place from which he might look out upon the imperfect world. It would have to be along the walls. And in the walls the windows or balconies would, for reasons of symmetry, be in the center. I went to the wall that faced the palace square, and at the center, far above the floor of the clock room, reached by many flights of stairs, was a door that led to a balcony. There, facing away from me, was the tutor, looking across the kingdom, backlit by rose-colored light from below.

Though up there we were enclosed in cloud and fog, and he looked like a man standing in front of a dense waterfall, I knew that his memory allowed him to survey the kingdom through the barriers that now obscured it, and that this was what he was doing. Somehow, he knew I was there, so he turned. The minute I saw his face, I ran to him, and he took me in his arms. For queen or not, blood or not, I was his child.

In the long telling of what had happened to me I discovered that, in choosing word by word what to say, I grew up. Yes, it was early, and it was magical, but often it is with kings and queens, as you yourself may discover. In summarizing to the tutor my course through the kingdom I had inherited and not yet claimed, I found that the important things rose as if under their own power, and that my tale was, surprisingly, one of equanimity and affection.

"I understand this," he said. "As you know, I have had occasion to look back myself."

"Why is it," I asked, "that some things now seem lovely and just that not long ago were so forbidding?"

"My dear Queen, for the teller of the tale, gratitude, love, and hope remain, because no matter what the story, its teller lives."

"Is that all?"

"No. It is also your duty to look with a loving eye upon all you have been given. This is what you have done, and you have done well."

I bowed my head and briefly closed my eyes. The tutor smiled, for he knew, though I did not, that this is how a queen acknowledges what is required of her.

"More to the point," he continued, "is what is to come. Events are unfreezing, and things are rising upon the wind."

"What events?" I asked. "Nothing here changes but for the worse. What can be done?"

"What must be done," he replied, "is to lead the Damavand generals from slavery and hiding. When they emerge en masse even with their ill-equipped and half-trained troops, they will be a match for the usurper's armies, and if they survive the first battles, they will triumph."

"Why haven't they done this before?" I asked. "They're only getting older."

"They cannot emerge until they have a leader, and a leader has not arisen among them. Of leaders you will find two kinds—those who choose themselves and those who are chosen. Whereas the first cannot but fail all tests after they come to power, the chosen strengthen from crisis to crisis. The paradox of the Damavand generals is that were any one to lead the others from slavery he would weaken, for the very act of proffering himself would be his demise.

"The Damavand," he said, "have been waiting for their chosen leader. They have been waiting . . . for you."

"For me?"

"This, my dear Queen, is the profession of a queen."

"But I have done nothing," I protested.

"Precisely," he continued. "You are the only one fit to lead, for you have been born to it, and it is a responsibility that you must bear rather than the prize you seek. The usurper stole your throne, and he cannot rule justly. You, on the other hand, having been lifted there gently, reluctantly, are still in possession of heart, humility, and justice."

"But I'm ten years old," I said. "How am I to lead generals from slavery?"

"Though the first steps will take your breath away," he told me, "they will not be difficult. Only subsequently, in the wars that follow, when the task of commanding the armies falls upon you, and you find the great Damavand generals hanging on your every word, will it be truly difficult. But I have faith in you: I know you will succeed."

"What are the first steps?" I asked.

He turned to look at the clouds of ferociously blowing snow, rose-colored from the fires below, with edges of gold and sparklings of diamond.

"Pray that it clears," he said. "For all will be lost if, two days from now, the sky is obscured by cloud."

"Upon this the kingdom rests?"

"Kingdoms rest upon lesser things and far more unlikely than just a clear day. Kingdoms are like the life of a man. No matter how vigorous they may seem, they hang by threads. Know this for the time that will come when you have cut the usurper's threads and hang by your own."

"What of the clear day?" I asked, wanting to hear.

The tutor nodded his head slowly, as if he were hoping. "The scholars of the kingdom will receive a signal, doubly confirmed, that you are alive and that you have returned."

"How will that be?" I asked. "The usurper controls all schedules, movement, and communication. Because he spreads rumors to cloud the truth, nothing can be believed. Do you know that I have heard that my father was a devil, that when he died he became a bird? That my mother died in the city, upon the lake, in the mountains, among the clouds?"

"A way exists to cut through all that. I designed it before I left. I passed it to the scholars, of whom, in my way, I was one, for it is their job, by definition, to seek and serve the truth."

"No longer," I told him. After all, he had just arrived, and I had been in the city for what seemed like years. "They serve the usurper now, and are in league with the Duke of Tookisheim. They have become flatterers and liars and fools. The usurper emptied half the asylums and scattered the inmates throughout the universities like chocolate chips."

"Really," he said.

"Yes."

"But, you see," he continued, "this business of being a scholar goes back quite a long way. Its root is very deep, and it may have more life than you think. I am sure that many real scholars are left and that new ones will be created by the very process of their search for truth, and that they will shrug off the flattery and coercion of the Duke of Tookisheim and the usurper as a deer shrugs off the rain—with a little flick.

"They will know what to look for and how to read it, and when.

They will inform the Damavand generals, who will gather in the palace square when the time is right. On that day the market will be more crowded than ever before. If the usurper is told of this he will delight at the strength of the economy. But!"

"But what?" I asked.

"In the square will be a thousand Damavand generals, each with a troop of a thousand dismounted cavalry. Multiply, my Queen, to see how many of your soldiers will be gathered to hear your first command."

"A million," I said, unable even to imagine such a sight.

"A million," he confirmed.

"But only a few hundred Damavand generals were taken into slavery."

"They were instructed that upon the loss of the kingdom they should tend to their numbers for the day that would come, and they have. In slavery and in exile, they have restored themselves to their original strength. They lack only practice and complete armament."

"Who gave those instructions?"

"I did, on your behalf. I had the emperor's seal. Not that overwrought diamond-encrusted serpent thing the usurper uses," the tutor said, "but the original imperial seal. Even those who have never seen or heard of it, when they look upon it, understand what it is. It's right here," he said, lifting up his leather satchel and removing the seal. "It belongs to no one but you."

The beauty of the seal was overwhelming. Three dolphins arched over an agitated sea on an oval of gold crowned by a crown. I looked above to see if a light were shining upon it and saw none, which was a surprise, for the seal sparkled as if in bright sun.

"It has been near you all your life. I kept it under a plank beneath your bed. It was your grandfather's, and his father's, and his father's father's, all the way back. Your father held it for a very short time, and looked at it as if it would not be his. I was there when he received it. I saw. Now you must take it without further thought, for it will be yours as long as you live."

I took it. "Will I use this, then, to prove myself to the Damavand generals in the palace square?"

"No. The power flows from you to the seal, not vice versa. You are the sovereign, not it. You must appear on the south balcony at the midpoint of the square, the one your grandfather used, and announce yourself."

"How will I be heard? My voice is small."

"Your voice will thunder, for they will be awaiting you. When you stand before them, the kingdom will electrify and your voice will carry to its remotest corners, never mind the square, which will shake as if beaten by bolts of lightning."

I could hardly believe this. "But when will I appear?" I asked.

"You will know to assume your destiny when the most humble and unlikely person in the kingdom understands as clearly as you and I what great things will occur, when all is drama, and you feel the moment flooding through your hands like the waters of a swollen thrashing stream."

Then I took leave of the tutor, the only father I had ever known. I assumed that he would be there on the great day of which he spoke, and that he would remain by my side thereafter, to guide me in the world he knew so much better than I.

He had said goodbye almost casually, though he had made his plans so long before that he must have worried that many of the people upon whom he depended would be dead. Though many were, and many shortly would be, quite a few remained, and they were devoted.

Just as the Damavand generals had been instructed to keep

their armies in the shadows, the scholars had been told, cryptically, that my return would be heralded by "a flaming angel from a dimming sun." For years, as scholars will, they debated the meaning of this phrase. Those who believed it literally became fewer and fewer. As time passed and an angel did not fall and the sun did not dim they were ridiculed, and they could not help but doubt themselves. In great tests, one always does: that is the test.

During the wars, and after, I was able to speak to them, and was not surprised to hear that, almost one and all, they had suspected that they were wrong, but they had believed nonetheless. The world of fact and event had seemed to conspire against them, for they had staked their hearts on miracles, and miracles were not forthcoming.

"Your Majesty," I was told, "I questioned my own faith so strongly that I despised myself for still believing, and, yet, I could not cease to believe, and I knew I would hold to my great expectation even on my dying day. I was prepared to go without the society of men and die alone, for everything in me said that God had spared the children, and that you would come back to us.

"My friends said, 'That is insanity,' and I answered, 'So it is, but it is also love, from which I will not stand down.' And, your Majesty, I gave up my life for this belief, not for any reward, but because of its beauty and its consistency."

Few were left to endure the discomforts of faith unproven and dreams unrealized. Nonetheless, when the day came, the few that were left were enough.

I did not think to question Astrahn and Notorincus when, after another long nocturnal flight under the limitless roof of the bakeries, they left me in the yam kitchens and rushed away. Though not until later was I to know where they were needed, I assumed that they had important business.

I was returned to the sorting apron as if in a dream, there to ponder which of my lives was real and which not. Had I been at the usurper's table? Had the tutor appeared? Had I ever lived in the South Mountains? Was I a queen? Was my parents' history what I believed? Or had I been working upon this apron for an eternity of madness and delusion?

The more time passed and the past receded, the more I lost faith, for in the end it is always the smallest things that can be grasped or proved that usurp our trust and focus our hearts—unless, by stubbornness and courage, we overcome them.

The days fled as one and none. I did not know if the air was clear or cloudy, and my heart sank when everything remained the same. For a week or two, and then a month, and longer, my hope remained alive. But then I bent my head, and my heart slept.

Unbeknownst to us as we labored in darkness, the sky had opened and the world was set in the sharp crystal that comes after a blizzard. The lake, I am told, was a royal blue ribbon, with waves that rose on high winds, and swift breeze-lines of foam. From the towers and pinnacles of city and palace the white rims of the mountains were scalloped in gold as the sun moved behind them and the gales blew the snow.

Astrahn and Notorincus had been summoned posthaste to a tannery in the poorest, most ferocious part of the city, the quarter where the usurper allowed criminals to take refuge as part of his design to keep the kingdom in a state of terror. He tolerated their outrages not from any sense of idiotic mercy but because, in truth, they were involved in the same enterprise and they had the same aim. The criminals viewed the mass of people as a herd to be culled, controlled, and coerced, and in this they were the usurper's natural allies.

Even Astrahn, a Damavand general who had fought the Golden Horde, feared this place and kept his hand upon the hilt of his sword. Needless to say, Notorincus, master baker and king of the Alpine Chocolate Truffle Brioche, who never had been a soldier and was almost as round as a cinnamon roll, trembled in fear.

On the worst hill of this unspeakable quarter, in its worst hollow, and on its worst street, sat the tannery, sunk in an unbearable smell. Here, slaves who were too repulsive to bring to the executioners labored at reducing carcasses and fats, and cured the hides and skins of skunks, weasels, and toads for the belts, wallets, and hats of the criminals who strutted about the quarter. Criminals then were fond of wearing hats of skunk fur, and not one wanted to be caught dead—as sometimes they were—without a toad-skin vest.

Disappearing among the fetid vats and retching as they picked their way over soft slimy floors, Astrahn and Notorincus were led to a tiny filth-encrusted hole in a back wall. A tannery slave pointed to it and said, "In there."

"In where?" Astrahn said, thinking of his clean tunic.

"In that hole you go."

"In that hole?"

"Yes. They all do."

"They do, do they?"

"Yes."

"And how is my friend here going to accomplish such a thing?"

The tannery slave looked over at Notorincus. "If bakery slaves suck in their stomachs and blow out all the air in their lungs we can push them through if we put some slime on the edges of the hole. We've done it before."

"But why should we go in there?" Notorincus asked.

"*I* don't know," the slave said. "You told us the password. People like you come here and tell us the password, and then they go in the hole."

"They do?"

"Every day. Sometimes a hundred a day. The hole used to be much smaller."

"What's in there?" Astrahn asked.

The slave shrugged his shoulders. "All I know is what the Duke of Tookisheim tells me."

This was the kingdom's most common expression, though young people had begun to say, "All I know is what Peanut

119

Tookisheim tells me." Peanut was slowly taking charge of the *Tookisheim Post*, and his first act had been to search out anyone who knew anything and kill him. Peanut's ambition was to be even stupider than his father, and, miraculously, he was succeeding.

"I think," Astrahn told Notorincus, "that we should wait until somebody comes out, and then we'll ask what's in there."

"No one ever comes out," the slave announced matter-of-factly.

"Really," Astrahn said.

"Never. Never happened."

Both Astrahn and Notorincus stared at the hole. "Well," said Astrahn, "we have our orders. Good bye, Notorincus."

"Good bye, Astrahn."

"You go first."

"No, you go first, you're thinner."

"You'll need me to push you."

"You were a soldier. I'm just a baker."

Astrahn cleared his throat and looked archly at Notorincus. "Feet first or head first?"

Ten minutes later, after a ride at tremendous speeds along the perfectly smooth course of a river of hot mineral water, Astrahn and Notorincus, who had been unable to utter a word

but had managed to grab one another's clothing, found themselves plummeting over a fall.

When they surfaced they were in an underground lake, and coming toward them over its steaming waters was a trim rosewood boat rowed by four Damavand soldiers. Standing in the prow, with a boat hook, was a Damavand lieutenant. Astrahn could hardly believe his eyes, for they were in full uniform, and the colors and emblems they wore without a thought were those he had not seen since the fall of the kingdom.

Even as he still floated, his hope and pride flooded back. "I am Astrahn," he said, "general of the First Corps of the Fifteenth Wave of Damavand cavalry." When the lieutenant dropped the boat hook and saluted as of old, Astrahn's heart was made young.

This was the Damavand high command, deep under the palace, a hundred levels below the gushing mineral springs that the usurper's soldiers thought were the bottom layer, beneath the tunnels of the rats and amid the water-choked seams in the rock. Here was the heart of the rebellion, where the Damavand generals carried on their work. And of all this, the monstrous key guides had not the faintest clue.

When Astrahn was led into the presence of the commander of the armies, he saluted stiffly, but his eyes held tears, for he and the commander had served together against the Golden Horde and in the Great War That Was Lost, and Astrahn had thought he was dead.

"Astrahn," the general said. "I need not tell you how good it is to see you again."

"Sir."

"But I have orders for you that must be carried out on the instant. You are to take a detachment of five swordsmen and archers to the tower, where you will secure the entrance, the stairs, and the clock room. The regent, guardian of the sovereign queen, is there alone. It is your honor to protect him."

"The queen lives?" Astrahn asked, electrified.

"We don't know, but the regent has called for the scholars to assemble in the palace square, and they are doing so at this very moment."

Newly clothed in the uniform of a Damavand general, Astrahn took the five soldiers and Notorincus, who wore the Damavand Civilian Assistance Crest, through one of the many exits from the underground chambers. They emerged from beneath the peacock shelters near the clock tower, bumping their heads and collecting straw as they ducked from under the roofs. Mothers and children were stunned to see soldiers who were not in black, but in the white and blue that they had thought they would never see again.

As the detachment double-timed through the winding streets to reach the tower, merchants ran to their windows and their patrons stood stock still. It was beyond hope, so far beyond hope that in the heart of each person to witness the passing of these soldiers rose the same refrain: "It cannot be. It cannot be . . ."

But it was, and just before one of the last alleys opened upon the square they encountered twelve soldiers of the usurper's royal guard, who had been on their way from the square to a ceremony for the Lord Mayor of the Lake.

"What?" the commander said as he saw the Damavand soldiers in blue and white. "Is this for a play?"

The answer arrived before he or a single one of his men could unsheathe their swords or lift their crossbows. Astrahn called out the orders of old, as if ten years had passed not in the bakeries but at the margin of the Veil of Snows, in battle against the Golden Horde.

"Archers load," he said, still holding the pace, for Damavand soldiers did not need to stop to fire their arrows, having learned to do so at a gallop.

In a flash, five Mongol bows somersaulted over the backs of the soldiers and into their hands, followed by fifteen arrows, one set on each bow and two draped between the fingers ready to be set.

"Aim and release," Astrahn said with the dispassion that he had learned from a lifetime on the frontier, and five solid arrows from the Mongol bows found the hearts of five soldiers.

The others, for years astoundingly brave when they had no enemy, fumbled with their weapons in fear, for they were used to cutting down unarmed men and capturing women and children for the selections. Though the sight of their uniforms was in itself capable of freezing an untrained opponent, their years of strutting and posing had paralyzed their ability to fight. And to their credit they understood that this, the first engagement of the next great war, was theirs to lose. The arrows found their marks, and thus the war began, though for many weeks the usurper's armies would find no one to fight, even though they would search the kingdom for soldiers in blue and white.

And by the time I appeared on the balcony the usurper's armies would have stood down, thinking that only six Damavand soldiers and a bakery slave had been the cause of their fright, and that all was safe. But when a million soldiers in the palace square would throw off the maroon cloaks of slavery to meet the sun with a prairie of blue and white as far as the eye could see, the usurper's generals would swallow hard.

Astrahn's men reached the tower unseen, entered, and closed the door behind them. They set up their defensive positions at the choke points on the stairs. When this was done, Astrahn climbed to the clock room, and there he found the tutor, who was attending to a figure of an angel, a life-sized construction of straw and wood and wax, that stood on the platform at the top of the stairs that led to the balcony. Had the tutor been anyone but the regent of the realm, Astrahn would have asked about the angel, but he bowed instead.

"Your Majesty," he said.

The tutor, who would nervously glance at the thousands of scholars assembling below, and then at the figure of the angel, was not pleased. "I'm just the regent," he told Astrahn. "Save that for the queen."

"The queen lives?"

"The queen lives." The tutor was preoccupied, Astrahn later told me. He had several cans of paraffin that he would bend to check, and then he would tap the angel, and look up at the hands of the huge clock above them. Astrahn hardly took notice of this, so shocked was he to hear that the queen was alive.

"Where?" Astrahn asked.

"In the yam kitchens."

"In the yam kitchens? The queen is in the yam kitchens!"

"Astrahn," the tutor said irritably, "you have been watching over her."

Astrahn was mute for at least a minute, and then he said, "You mean, you mean, that little moppet? The ragamuffin? The forest girl?"

"Yes."

"Who works on the sorting apron, whom we took to the dinner?"

"Yes! Yes!"

"She's the queen. The little girl?"

"She's your queen, general."

Overcome with emotion, Astrahn pulled himself out of his astonishment and said, quietly and resolutely, "The queen

128

lives. All these years, when they thought it was just a dream, it was true. God save the queen."

He was ready to fight now as never before, and he asked for his orders.

"It's now seventeen after two. Can you hold the tower until five past three?"

"If the tower is stormed, we'll do our best."

"You must. Five after three. Hold 'til then, and the kingdom is saved."

Later, Astrahn told me that when he left the regent he saw in his eyes the reflection of the kingdom, marvelously clear, with the sky above and the clouds scudding by like ships.

In the square below, many thousands of scholars had assembled. Because their rivalries prevented them from associating with one another, they were spread out with remarkable evenness. And as they were naturally timid and not a single one was ignorant of the cavalry sweeps, they tended to stay near the exits. This placement, which he had foreseen, suited the tutor's purposes exactly.

A relatively late arrival at the eastern end of the square was the astronomer Jopincus, a flatterer of the Duke of

Tookisheim, whom the Duke of Tookisheim flattered in turn. Hundreds upon hundreds of articles in the *Tookisheim Post* had been devoted to the brilliant Jopincus and his "obviously correct" theory that, if the people did not do exactly what the usurper and the Duke of Tookisheim told them to do, the sun would explode.

And more thousands of articles in the *Tookisheim Post*, on subjects as varied as the self-esteem of female merry-go-round attendants, or the most prestigious way to glaze a mushroom, would begin nonetheless with the words, "Experts agree," or, "It is beyond question," or, "No mainstream scientist would question," followed by "that if everyone does not heed the instructions of the emperor and the Duke of Tookisheim, the sun will explode."

The phrases, "All I know is what the Duke of Tookisheim tells me," and, "All I know is what Peanut Tookisheim tells me," had soon been joined by another: "Do what the emperor says, or the sun will explode."

Jopincus hung back at the eastern end of the square, wondering why the scholars had been turned out when there was no imperial holiday. And he kept checking the clock in the tower, for he knew he would have to leave soon were he to return to his observatory in time to record the full eclipse of the sun at five after three.

Then he caught a glimpse of the tutor, high in the tower, and he put the disparate elements together. As quickly as he could, he ran to find the usurper.

Of course, no one ever knew the usurper's whereabouts, and had Jopincus gone all the way to the headquarters of the Imperial Guard as he had set out to do, he would not have arrived until it was too late. But as he was crossing the Avenue of the Ravens he saw a column of two thousand imperial troops riding toward him, and at their center was the usurper in his chariot.

They would have killed Jopincus merely for blocking their way, had he not been known throughout the kingdom and had he not screamed again and again, "Tell the emperor that I am the astronomer Jopincus and I have an urgent message for him!"

The usurper was, if anything, quick to see a plot, and within a few minutes of receiving Jopincus he wheeled his column about and thundered back down the Avenue of the Ravens toward the tower.

His soldiers ferociously besieged the stairs, and for fifteen minutes Astrahn and his men fought the most difficult battle of their lives. They could not hold the door, which had been immediately blasted open with gunpowder. And though each of their arrows found the heart of one of the Imperial Guard, their stock was soon exhausted and they were able to fire only those shafts that they could retrieve from the cluttered and blood-stained ground on which they fought. In retrieving, they were unduly exposed, and they fell, one by one, until all were killed except Astrahn and Notorincus, who, as the clock struck three, were ten flights from the top with not a single arrow and only Astrahn's sword left with which to fight.

Then a shot rang out, and Astrahn fell. He turned to Notorincus: "Get to the top of the stairs. Protect the regent."

"I have no weapons," Notorincus said, in absolute terror. "What shall I do?"

"Divert them. It's only a matter of minutes. Go!"

Notorincus began the fast climb up ten flights of stairs, with arrows and crossbow bolts clanging in the railings and against the treads all around him. "I'll never bake another waffle-torte for a single imperial soldier as long as I live!" he said, which was his cry of battle.

Just before the top of the stairs he looked down and saw

the soldiers chaining Astrahn before leading him away. Others were flying up the stairs.

Notorincus slammed the clock room door behind him. It had only a small latch, which he set. But as he set it he saw in his mind's eye the metal exploding apart as the door was forced. He hit the door with the heel of his hand and shouted, "No eclairs, you idiots!"

Then he turned toward the balcony landing. The tutor was looking down at him. He had a can of paraffin in one hand and a flaming torch in the other. "Are you all that's left?" the tutor asked.

"Yes, sir," Notorincus answered.

"You're not a soldier."

"No, sir. I'm a baker."

"Can you hold them for two minutes? You don't even have a weapon."

"No, sir, I don't, but I can try to hold them." He turned and looked fearfully toward the sound of boots on the stairs.

"And how do you propose to do that?"

"Ah, well, uh, oh boy, uh, oh," Notorincus said as the first chain-mailed shoulders began to slam against the door. He moved away, toward a looped chain that was rising far into the clock mechanism high above. This was a lift for mechanics, who could exit at many different levels merely by stepping off the rising chain onto little aerial platforms. Thence they could take winding tunnels amid the gears and shafts of light, the cylinders, and the wheels, that ran the clock.

"I'll distract them," Notorincus said, slowly rising, "by taunting them."

The tutor seemed skeptical.

With an explosive burst of sound the door flew open and metal jangled to the floor. Half a dozen soldiers flooded in, stopped, and looked about. They didn't see Notorincus, but they did see the tutor soaking the angel with paraffin. "That's the one!" a soldier said, but as they began to lurch in the direction of the balcony stairs, Notorincus cleared his throat.

"Ahagghham!" he said. "I am the regent of the realm, and here I am, rising up to a rather secret place where I will be able to work a machine that will give your emperor fits."

"You're just a fat slave."

"No. I'm the regent. You don't know that I'm the regent because you're too stupid to walk frontward. Tell me, have you taken your stupid pills today, or did your mother swallow the whole bottle?"

The soldiers were livid. They cranked their crossbows. "Oh," said Notorincus. "Let's see. You think you can hit me at this distance? Most soldiers could put a bolt through the lattice of an apple pullover, but you couldn't hit a spread-eagled hippopotamus."

By now the sun had begun to dim. The tutor was ready to carry the angel to the balcony rail, but he was watching Notorincus slowly rise, and he saw the soldiers lift their crossbows. "I'm the regent!" he shouted. "Not he. Come for me."

"Shut up, old man! We have half a dozen bolts to put in the heart of a slave."

Notorincus cringed. He had nowhere to go. He closed his eyes, and smiled.

The tutor lit the angel and it blazed up bright with silver-gold flame. He bent to its feet and tumbled it over the rail—not of the balcony, as he had planned, but onto the soldiers. They screamed as it fell, and were consumed.

Amid the steady clanking of the machinery, almost at its heart, Notorincus opened his eyes. As he saw what had happened, those eyes filled with tears, for he knew that the regent of the realm had made the decision to give his life for that of a slave.

"Sir!" he called out as he saw the tutor bathing himself in the remaining paraffin. "Sir! Let *me*! Let *me*!" But eclipses do not last long, and the tutor, besides, was a man of honor who would never have allowed anyone to take his place.

"Tell the queen," the tutor said, "that I love her not because she is our queen, but because she is my daughter. Tell her that when she crosses to the other side of the Veil of Snows, I will be there to take her in my arms."

And then Notorincus watched the regent of the realm step to the rail, torch in hand, and he cried.

By the time the first detachment of soldiers reached the balcony, the tutor was already standing on the rail. They were too late. In a slow and graceful arc he bent the torch to touch his paraffin-soaked garments, and fell forward. As he hurtled through the air the wind made the flames flash. Upon seeing his flight through the dim light of the eclipse the scholars knew that the prophecy was real. They fled the square more quickly than the usurper's soldiers could seal it, and from them the word spread like fire.

They said that as he fell he flew, tumbling and wheeling in the air in slow motion, his arms outspread with all his strength, the fire trailing like the tail of a comet. When the people heard, they knew I had returned and that the kingdom was theirs. And the story of the falling angel would not leave them, for they all had known how my father and mother had died. They were forever moved by this, and, needless to say, so was I.

As word spread, as the armies mobilized, and as a series of blizzards crossed the lake, I was unaware. Laboring day after day in the yam kitchens, I was lost in the darkness and the cold. Had the government decided to send the kingdom's ten-year-old girls to selection I might easily have been caught in the sweeps, but the usurper believed that I had taken refuge in Dolomitia-Swift and would march upon the kingdom with armies raised abroad. He had no idea that within the city he had so carefully sealed, the armies that would defeat him were preparing to rise, or that I was hard at work in one of his forgotten kitchens. I am certain it never would have crossed his mind that the young queen he so feared bathed in yam water and (after I had left my room in the tower) slept on a wooden shelf in a room with forty girls who could neither read nor write.

We awoke in the hours before dawn, and although we could not see the stars, the wagon unloaders told us that early in the morning, when the fewest eyes were open, the stars were at their brightest and most beautiful.

We had only one kerosene lamp. Each day as we struggled to arise, our hands cracked with dryness, our clothes filthy, I would pull on my torn dress in the light of this lamp. Its fumes filled the room, and the ceiling was checkered with soot. The globe and chimney were long blackened, the wick ragged, and the flame broken, but every morning I came to the lamp, and though I shivered and I was sick and I thought there would be no end to my captivity, I saw that the flame, floating upon a level and invisible crystal of vaporized fuel, was pure. I could never find fault with it, or an imperfection in its color, even when all was weakening and all was lost and the world seemed forever dark.

The days and nights fused together in exhaustion. A weak hope would sometimes glint in a vast field of darkness, only to falter and disappear without a sound. Then, as I was working on the apron one morning, sometimes remembering the mountains, sometimes thinking not a single thought, the yams stopped rolling down, the lights flickered, and the machinery failed. Never before had this happened. For the first time, we could hear the sounds of boiling and frying beneath the boiling and frying chutes, and the muffled roars of the yam-eating whatever-they-were far below, and we looked at each other—that is, all the yam curling girls on the apron—and laughed.

Expecting the machinery to start up again, we waited patiently, leaning on our brooms. Nothing happened, so we sat down on the apron and rested. Having absorbed heat from the many fires below it, the iron floor was warm.

"What do you think it is?" one girl asked. I had never heard her speak.

"Perhaps one of the blizzards of February shut down the power-maker," another girl speculated.

"That can't be," said someone else. "The lights are on." And then she said, "You know, if ever I am not a yam curler, I will never look at another yam again. I *hate* yams!"

We laughed, and a freckled red-haired girl said, "You may

never look at one, but you'll have them in your dreams for the rest of your life."

Then we heard someone shouting from the far side of the apron: "Elena's coming! Elena's coming!"

We stood holding our brooms, feigning worry that we had no yams to curl.

"Elena, there are no yams," someone said when she arrived.

"It doesn't matter," Elena answered. "It doesn't matter. Come here, girls. Come to me."

We walked to the edge of the apron. Some of us jumped down. Others remained, holding on to the iron beams that crisscrossed above. We knew that something had happened, and that things had changed. I breathed lightly, waiting for her to speak, for I sensed that this might be the moment I had been waiting for all my life, even when I had not known it.

Elena looked into the faces and eyes of all the girls who had been on the apron since they were children. They knew nothing else, and this was clear from their expression. But their eyes also showed that they would sense, perhaps better than most, the rising of the wind.

"You think," she said, "that you will be here forever, don't you."

"Will we not?"

"No," she said. "Oh no. You must not think that. You must not despair."

"And why is that?" an older girl asked bitterly.

"You must not despair," Elena said, "for today we have been told a great thing. We have been told that it is true that the child was saved. Long ago, we thought our queen had died." Elena could hardly finish her sentence, and I myself was trembling as she continued. "But a great thing has happened, and this we know for sure. We are not abandoned. The queen has come back. She is among us. She lives."

I knew that this was the beginning, but I did not feel joy, for there was a man that I missed, and I miss him still today. Nonetheless, I had a job to do, and I knew I would be carried through on a long wave of the honor and courage of those who had come before me.

It happened exactly as the tutor had foreseen. After what seemed like an eternity, I finally stood at a closed door beyond which lay the open world and the palace square filled with a million of my soldiers, many of whom would soon give their lives in the fight against the usurper's massive armies.

Before I opened this door, on the other side of which were blue sky and the cold air of winter, I hesitated, for I knew that the simple act of opening it would unleash years of war. I knew that stepping forward meant that whole families would perish, never to be remembered, and that half the kingdom would burn.

But what we had was the same or worse: the deathly clouds of black smoke had never stopped billowing from the distant chimneys. So I prayed for guidance and called upon the memory of my murdered forebears, and when I did I felt their blood in my blood, their hearts in my heart. I pushed at the door. It opened. And all at once the blue sky came flooding in, and the millions in the square fell silent.

MARK HELPRIN was raised on the Hudson and educated at Harvard College, Harvard's Graduate School of Arts and Sciences, and the University of Oxford. He is the author of many books, including the best-selling *Winter's Tale*, and *A Soldier of the Great War*. He lives with his wife, Lisa, and their two daughters in upstate New York.

CHRIS VAN ALLSBURG was born in Grand Rapids, Michigan. He received his B.F.A. in sculpture from the University of Michigan and an M.F.A., also in sculpture, from the Rhode Island School of Design. He is the author of two Caldecott Medal winners, *The Polar Express* and *Jumanji*. He lives with his wife, Lisa, and their two daughters in Providence, Rhode Island.